# WITCH YOU WOULDN'T BELIEVE

## BELIEVE

### A LEMON TEA COZY MYSTERY

LUCY MAY

Copyright © 2018 Lucy May

All rights reserved.

ISBN: 1987455967

ISBN 13: 978-1987455960

Cover design by Cosmic Letterz

❀ Created with Vellum

# DEDICATION

*To magic, to my dogs & to coffee.*

**Sign up for my newsletter for information on new releases!**
*https://lucymayauthor.com/subscribe*

***Follow me!***
*https://www.facebook.com/lucymayauthor/*
*lucy@lucymayauthor.com*

# CHAPTER 1

"I'll be back tomorrow at the latest," I said to Tara, who was the assistant manager at my bakery and a good friend. "If you need anything, call my cell. Hopefully, they have decent service down there," I grumbled, thinking about the sleepy southern town where I grew up.

"Everything will be fine, just go," Tara said, pushing me out the door of my own shop. "I've got this. Go take care of your business."

I sighed, secretly wishing she would tell me she needed me to stay. I didn't want to go home. I'd left that place the day after I graduated and hadn't looked back in six years. Returning home had not been on my list of top one thousand things I wanted to do.

"Thank you. I'll check in once I know what's going on and why I need to be there," I said.

She giggled. "You know why. You own the factory, which we are going to talk about when you get back. You never told me you were a lemon tea tycoon."

"I'm not a tycoon. My grandmother loved her spiked lemon tea so much, she made it into a business. That factory hasn't been up and running since I was a kid. Everyone in town is convinced the old building is haunted. I'm surprised it hasn't collapsed into a pile of bricks by now."

"Why didn't your grandmother leave it to your mom?" she asked.

I shrugged and shook my head. "Because my grandma was crazy? I dunno actually. My grandma said it was my inheritance. I inherited a giant old factory building, and I have no idea what to do with it. My mom said she had her own house and didn't need my grandmother's, but it was my destiny to inherit. Did I ever tell you that my family is a tad on the wacky side?"

That drew another soft giggle from Tara. "*You* are a little out there. Go. Quit stalling."

"Fine, but I want it on the record that I don't want to go. I'm no Nancy Drew. I don't see how I can be of any help in a death investigation."

"*Murder* investigation, and you don't have to be the sleuth. That's what the cops are there for, but as owner of the building, you could be liable," she said with a sniff. "I think it's almost better for you if it is a murder instead of an accidental death. They can't hold you liable for someone murdering someone there."

"How would you know that?"

She grinned, "I watch lots of crime shows."

"Great. I'm two-hundred miles away, haven't stepped foot in that factory in almost twenty years and now I'm to blame for some guy getting himself killed in the place," I grumbled, grabbing my purse and heading for the front door.

"Try and have some fun!" Tara called out as I threw open the door to my little bakery, the bell jingling behind me.

I stomped down the street to my car, tossed in my purse and pointed the nose of the car south. I was going home.

Some people loved the idea of going home after being away for a while. Not me.

My heart was with my bakery and the new life I had forged for myself in Saint Anne, Louisiana. I loved my mom, but Lemon Bliss, Louisiana felt more like a prison than a real hometown to me. Growing up in the tiny town, I'd spent much of my time wondering about the world beyond its sleepy borders. When I had finally moved away, it had felt as if the world beyond it was gigantic and just waiting for me. Now, here I was, driving home—all because I'd inherited my grandmother's now-defunct lemon tea factory and a dead body had been found there.

With a sigh, I cranked up the stereo and settled in for the drive. Rolling down the window, I let my hair fly as I sped down the highway. The sooner I got there to resolve this, the sooner I could leave.

Three hours later, I was pulling into Lemon Bliss. The town got its name before my family's lemon tea factory brought the town out of obscurity. Several family farms had lemon orchards here, hence it became known as Lemon Bliss. My grandparents had founded the lemon tea factory in the early half of the twentieth century. My grandmother was known for her legendary lemon tea, made from the lemons grown on the family farm and spiked generously with vodka. Her tea was guaranteed to make you loopy and was a southern specialty. During its heyday in the middle of the century, the factory pumped out spiked lemon tea and sold it like crazy for a few decades. After my grandfather passed away when I was a little girl, my grandmother had closed it down. The factory had sat idle since then.

There were no stoplights and only one main road through town, Crooked Street. Very original. I stared ahead at the crooked oak tree at the end of the street. The tree had been there for centuries. It was a southern live oak tree. I'd yet to grasp the difference between a live oak and a regular

3

oak tree, but I digress. The entire town had been built around the tree. No one dared cut down the ancient tree that was as crooked as a question mark. Rumor had it the tree had been hit by lightning, split and nearly fell over, but it was still growing, albeit crooked.

I parked my car along the almost-empty street and headed into what you might refer to as the town headquarters. Crooked Coffee was the place to be. It was the post office, deli, gossip hub, coffee shop and then some. Having lived away for years, I'd forgotten how good this place was. The moment I pushed through the screen door, I was assailed with the scent of fresh coffee and baked bread. I was starving and needed sustenance before I tracked down the sheriff who'd called me about the body found in the factory.

Glancing around, I saw that the place was busy even though it was late afternoon. I threaded through the small round tables scattered about the place and stopped in front of the counter. "Hi," I said, grabbing the attention of the lone employee.

"Is that you Violet Broussard?"

I glanced around, following the high-pitched voice that rang out across the coffee shop. I froze. I hadn't contemplated how to deal with running into anyone. My eyes landed on Lila Montgomery, a friend of my mother's as she made her way from the door to me. I silently sighed. I wasn't up for being grilled, but I'd best get ready.

"Why yes it is. I knew it. I could spot you from anywhere," Lila said as she reached my side.

I took a deep breath, pasted on a smile and turned to her. "Hi, Lila."

"Why, look at you, dear. You are just as beautiful as your mother, sweetie," she replied. Lila looked mostly as I'd remembered—still thin and spry with bright blue eyes. Her once dark hair was now gray with a lavender due, as if her stylist was a touch off with the coloring.

"Thank you, Lila," I said, turning around to face the deli counter, again.

I wasn't going to get off that easy. She remained at my side as I ordered a sandwich and coffee. "Are you here because of that unfortunate business at the factory?" she said in a low, conspiratorial tone.

I should have known Lila would have the 4-1-1 on anything happening in Lemon Bliss.

"Sheriff Smith called and asked me to come down," I answered.

Lila rolled her eyes. "Oh, Harold, always making a big to-do about everything. Unless," she said leaning closer, "unless he thinks foul play is involved. I hear it was murder, but who would ever do such a thing?"

"I have no idea. I'm just hoping I can get things taken care of and get back home," I said, paying for my sandwich and coffee.

"Oh, dear, your mom misses you something fierce. You should visit more often. She'll be so happy to see you in town, where you belong."

"It's difficult to visit regularly. I own my own business and can't always get away," I explained, a little tersely.

Lila reached out a hand and touched my hair. "You look so much like your mother. That black hair is so pretty. I always envied your mama's hair."

I leaned back, managing a smile. Lila was eccentric, even more so than my mother, which was pretty hard to beat.

"Thank you, Lila, but I need to go find the sheriff."

She tsk-tsked me. "That is some nasty business. Murder. In our little town. Who'd have thought? It's a real whodunit."

"I don't know if anyone knows it was murder just yet," I

reminded her. "The sheriff said he just has some questions about the factory."

She nodded her head. "Mm-hmm, I bet he does. He's always been nosey about that place and us for that matter," she said, under her breath.

"What does you mean?" I asked.

"Lila, are you bothering this poor woman?" a strange man stepped towards us, interrupting the conversation.

My attention was immediately drawn to him. He was new in town. Well, maybe not new, new, but he hadn't been around when I'd moved away.

"Oh, Gabriel, you flirt," Lila cooed, slapping his arm playfully. "Gabriel, sweetie, this is our lovely Violet. You know her mama, Virginia. The Broussard women are one of the oldest families in town. In fact, her great-grandmother was one of the founders, really. That old lemon tea factory? Honey, you're looking at the owner."

Gabriel looked at me and I fell into his wide blue eyes. The man was far too handsome for his own good. With sandy blonde hair, a strong, square jaw, and a dimple in his cheek when he smiled, sweet Jesus he sent a little flutter through me.

"The owner of the lemon tea factory!" he said, with feigned excitement, obviously meant as sarcasm. "I'm Gabriel Trahan, pleased to meet you," he said, extending his hand. "It isn't everyday you meet Lemon tea royalty."

"You must be new to town," I commented as I shook his hand.

ANOTHER ONE OF those thousand-watt smiles. "Good point. I moved here last year. My aunt Coral lives here."

"Then I'll forgive you for not bowing to royalty," I quipped. "What kind of work do you do?"

His mouth curled at one corner in a flirty grin that made

me instantly think he was trouble. I didn't want or need trouble. "I'm kind of a jack of all trades. I fix things, build things, whatever needs doing, I do."

"He's really a very helpful young man in a town full of women of a certain age," Lila said with a big smile.

I dropped his hand. "I have to get going. It was nice to meet you, Gabriel. Good to see you, Lila."

"Oh, now, don't run off," Lila cajoled.

"Lila, I need to get moving. I promised Sheriff Smith I'd go straight to his office."

"The sheriff?" Gabriel chimed in, his dark blonde eyebrows hitching up.

That was all the invitation Lila needed. The woman was a world-class gossip. I couldn't remember a time when she wasn't talking about someone doing something, or sharing details of something happening in town. She was a hub of information.

"Yes," she drawled out in her exaggerated southern accent. "Violet, here, owns that big ol' factory on the other side of town. A man was found dead inside. The sheriff suspects foul play."

Gabriel looked at me. It wasn't surprise I was reading in those endless blue eyes. It was something else, but I couldn't put my finger on it.

I rolled my eyes, "We don't actually know anything yet. Lila has a very vivid imagination."

"That sounds…uh, surprising. The factory is abandoned, right?" Gabriel asked.

I shrugged, "I don't know about abandoned, but it's been empty for years."

He nodded, holding my gaze. "If it was empty, how did anyone know there was a body inside?"

Lila winked. "That's a good question. It's a mystery."

"You're only encouraging her," I told him.

He chuckled. "Sorry. I have to be going. Good to see you

again, Lila." He turned his gaze back to me. His scrutiny made me squirm a little. "Maybe I'll see you around."

"I'll be leaving as soon as I talk to the sheriff," I shot back.

"Too bad," he grinned and left the building.

Lila was looking at me with eyes that saw too much. Sometimes, I almost believed the rumors about her being a witch.

"You know that sheriff wants to blame it on us. Well, your mom, anyway. He's always had it out for all of us," she clucked, shaking her head.

"What are you talking about, Lila? Why would he blame my mother for murder?"

She grabbed my arm and pulled me into the corner of the room. "Because we're witches," she whispered. "He's convinced we're responsible for anything that happens in this town."

"Oh, Lila."

"It's time, sweetie," she whispered.

"Time for what?" I asked, growing more confused by the minute.

She stood up to her full height and looked directly into my eyes. "Violet, it's time for you to take your position as leader. It's time to pass on the torch from mother to daughter."

Lila wasn't that old. She was my mother's age, but obviously, she had dementia. "Leader of what?"

"The coven."

"What? Lila, you've been watching too much TV."

She put her hands on her hips and stared me down. "No, I haven't. It's time, Violet. We've all waited long enough. It's time."

With a shake of my head and a laugh, I walked out of the building. I wasn't about to entertain her crazy nonsense.

# CHAPTER 2

*I* drove straight over to the small building that housed the city hall and the sheriff's office. The sheriff wasn't in, which only fed my impatience. I had driven three hours to talk to him in person and the man didn't have the decency to wait for me.

"When will he be back?" I asked the elderly woman who acted as his secretary and dispatcher of sorts.

"Why, I couldn't say. He got called out to old Mrs. Blankenship's place. Someone broke into her root cellar, again."

I nodded my head in understanding. It was the same call she made every week since as long as I could recall. The woman had been senile since I was a little girl. She was convinced someone broke in and stole all her homemade jelly. Every week. When I was a teen, we had staked out the root cellar on more than one occasion to see if we could catch the culprit. We never did, and it wasn't long before I started to suspect the theft was all in Mrs. Blankenship's head.

"Thank you. Can you please tell him Violet Broussard stopped by and I'm hoping to talk with him soon?"

The woman smiled. "I know who you are dear. I'll tell him just as soon as he gets back. Will you be staying at your grandmother's house?"

"I suppose I'll have to," I managed. What I'd hoped to be an afternoon trip was looking like it would definitely be more than that.

"I'll let him know you were here," she said. "I stopped by to smell the flowers at your grandmother's house the other day. It's like she is still there, tending those beautiful roses," she said, wistfully.

I nodded, wondering if she was also going a little senile. "Glad they are still blooming."

"Oh, sweetie. They are the talk of the town. I think she bewitched them."

"Bewitched who?" I asked, suddenly on guard after what Lila had said.

"The flowers. No one has that green of a thumb. I imagine it was one of her magic spells that made them so pretty."

*Okaaaay.* "All right, well, I guess I'll go check on the house and those flowers. Please let the sheriff know I'm short on time and would rather get this all done and over with as soon as possible."

The woman giggled, "You know Harold. The man likes to take his sweet time doing anything."

Clamping my jaw shut, I bit back my retort. I knew that, which was why I'd been reluctant to drive down here in the first place. Lemon Bliss and its people moved as slow as molasses. I had better things to do than sit here and wait around for the sheriff to ask questions I couldn't possibly answer anyway.

Beating back my annoyance, I walked back to my car.

Harold Smith, Lemon Bliss's one and only sheriff, had all but ordered me to get down here and then he wasn't even around to ask me the questions he claimed were too important to go over on the phone.

"Dangit!" I muttered, once inside the safety of my car.

Staring out the windshield, I debated what to do. It was just about spring and a cluster of azaleas was filled with buds in the front of the police station. Scanning the area, I took in the quiet downtown with its picturesque store fronts, sidewalks lined with flowerboxes soon to be awash with blooms, trees scattered along the streets creating a canopy of shade, and a few people strolling along the sidewalks. Lemon Bliss was a quiet, peaceful town. If you didn't know it was the year 2018, you could easily land here and wonder if it were 1950. Not much had changed. Oh, the residents weren't stuck in the past or anything. It was just that Lemon Bliss was far enough away from any urban areas, it stayed quiet and people liked it that way.

When my stomach growled, I remembered my sandwich and quickly scarfed it down, hoping Harold would return by the time I was finished. He didn't. So, I guess it was off to my grandma's house. Or my house, rather. I had inherited the Victorian home along with the factory. I had debated the merits of selling it, but couldn't bring myself to do it. It felt wrong. My mother didn't want it, citing my destiny and all that jazz. She was living hers, and I had to live mine. More of my mother's wild ramblings.

I drove to the edge of town, past the crooked oak tree and towards my grandma's home. I could see the factory in the distance. Seeing the old, gray building that stood sentry over the town sent a shiver down my spine. The place had always given me the creeps. It was a massive old place in a town filled with two-story homes and quaint buildings. Nothing else was nearly as big as that factory.

As I pulled into the driveway of the big, Victorian home, I stared. The flowers were growing out of control. Thousands of colorful flowers covered the yard, snaked up the covered porch rails and completely swallowed the small white picket fence I knew I had passed when I pulled in.

"Wow!" I exclaimed, staring at the vivid explosion of color. Now I understood what the secretary had been talking about. It was an amazing display that would make any gardener envious.

I was going to have to send the caretaker I hired a special thank you note. I had never seen such healthy, abundant flowers. That person deserved the credit, not some silly rumor about witchcraft.

Climbing out of my car, I walked up onto the front porch. Grandma's favorite wooden rocking chair was still there. It didn't look the least bit worn. I sat down, inhaling the scent of the flowers and smiling, thinking of my grandmother. I missed her.

I pulled out my phone, hoping I would have a signal, and called Tara.

"Hi!" she greeted. "Don't tell me you're already on your way back!"

I chuckled, "I wish. No, looks like I'm going to have to stay the night," I said, checking my watch. "The sheriff got called out. I'm waiting to talk to him, but the man isn't exactly efficient," I explained with a sigh.

"Oh, I'm sorry, but it'll give you time to visit your mom at least, right?"

I cringed. I knew my mom would lecture me about not visiting. "Yes, I suppose."

"Is there like a haunted hotel you get to stay in?" she asked, excitedly.

"No, I'll be staying in my grandma's house. My house," I corrected, still unable to accept ownership of the beautiful place.

"You own a house?" she asked, her tone shocked.

"Yes. It was my grandmother's. She willed it to me."

"Holy cow! I didn't know you were loaded. I think we need to be better friends," she teased. "Your grandmother left you everything?"

"Yes. My mom did get a sizeable cash inheritance, but everything else came to me." I left out the part about me receiving the bulk of her fortune. I didn't like people to know that. "Trust me, if you saw what I inherited, you would be running the opposite direction."

"I doubt that. Is it a big house?"

I turned to look at the house behind me. "I guess. It's old. It was built at the turn of the twentieth century. My grandma modernized it somewhat, but not a lot. It has four bedrooms, all on the small side, and two bathrooms."

"That sounds amazing. Take pictures! I want to see it," she laughed. "Is it haunted?"

"What is with you and haunted houses?"

"You know I love that stuff. I can't wait until Halloween. I've got plans to go to New Orleans this year. Don't forget, I'll be gone that whole week," she reminded me for what had to be the tenth time. Halloween was months away, but she planned ridiculously far in advance.

"I know, I know, you crazy woman. One of these days you'll realize all that stuff is nonsense."

"Nope. Never. I believe in the supernatural. You should too," she said decidedly. "There are all kinds of creatures that walk among us. All you have to do is believe."

I hated talk of that kind of stuff. It hit a little too close to home since I had grown up under a cloud of suspicion. There had always been rumors around town about my mother and grandmother. I always reminded my friends that I would be the first to know if the rumors were true. But it didn't help. Nothing ever stopped the gossip from periodically making the rounds.

"I don't believe a bit of it," I told her, meaning it. "How's everything going there?" I said, pointedly changing the subject.

She giggled. "Everything is fine here. Relax and enjoy your visit. Oh, I have a customer coming in, better run. Call me as soon as you know something. I have to live vicariously through you!"

Rolling my eyes, I hung up the phone. So glad someone was enjoying this mess. I fished out the set of keys I'd been carrying around for years, though I'd never used them. They had come in the mail, along with the deed to the house and factory. I had hired a caretaker when my mother refused to keep an eye on things for me, saying it was my responsibility. I had taken great satisfaction in hiring the caretaker. That showed her.

"Here goes nothing," I muttered, expecting layers of dust, cobwebs everywhere, and furniture covered with sheets.

I pushed open the front door and stood stalk still. I couldn't move.

The house was exactly as Grandma had left it. I could almost smell the scent of fresh baked bread coming from the old kitchen. Once again, I reminded myself to send the caretaker a note. The home was in immaculate condition.

The gleaming mahogany floors had been waxed and polished to a high sheen. My fingers trailed over the arm of one of the antique couches that faced two antique armchairs. All were clean, without a speck of dust. I made my way through the sitting room and into the kitchen where I had many fond memories of baking with my grandmother.

I stood in the kitchen and closed my eyes. I could practically feel her there, her hands busy kneading dough on the large butcher block on the center island. I could smell the yeast mingled with the ever-present scent of lemon in the air and hear her voice as she told me stories while she worked. I missed her terribly.

"I thought I'd find you here," my mother's voice cut through the vivid memory.

I spun around, startled to see her. "Hi, you scared me."

"Were you spending some quality time with your grandmother?" she asked, completely serious.

That was my mom. Spirit communicator. "No, I was just remembering baking in here with her. It always smelled like bread and lemons and it still does."

She nodded with a knowing smile. "She's here."

"What?"

"You can feel her. You have to admit that, Violet. Every time I come here, I can feel her. Close your eyes and open your mind."

I shrugged. I didn't have to admit anything. My mom was the daft one who did the spirit thing. Not me.

"Have you been keeping the place up?" I asked, suddenly wondering if my mom had changed her mind.

"No. I came by earlier today and put fresh linens on the bed and removed those horrible sheets from the furniture. I wanted it to be ready for you. Those sheets make it look so drab in here. I hate those things. Why does that man insist on covering the furniture with them?"

"To protect the furniture. It isn't like anyone sees how drab it looks," I countered.

"Well, you would, which is why I pulled them off."

"I hadn't actually planned on coming here at all."

She ignored my comment. "I brought you some things," she said, holding up a couple of bags.

"Like?"

"A few groceries and toiletries. I didn't think you would have remembered to pack those with you."

"Thank you. I didn't. I hadn't planned on staying the night," I reiterated.

One of her perfectly sculpted black brows lifted. "What do you mean? Of course, you'll stay."

"I was hoping to answer the questions the sheriff had and go home tonight. I don't want to stay here any longer than I have to."

"Violet, don't you see? This is an omen. It's time for you to come home," she said, walking towards me, her charm bracelets softly tinkling as she moved. "Your grandmother left you the house so you could live here and raise your own daughter here."

My ears focused on the clinking of her bracelets, blocking out what she was saying. With both my mother and my grandmother wearing clusters of bracelets while I was growing up, the sound reminded me of my childhood. It took me back to a simpler time. A time before I had to be an adult and give up the wistful fantasies my mother and grandmother were always spinning.

I blinked a few times, nearly hypnotized by the charms. "Mom, I'm not staying. I have a life and a business to get back to. This isn't my home anymore."

She turned and started unpacking the bags. Her back was to me, so I couldn't see the expression on her face, but I didn't need to see it to know she was upset.

"I thought you would be staying. This is important, Violet. We need you."

"What is so important?"

She turned around to look at me. "Us. Me. The girls. The sheriff has some ideas about what he thinks may have happened in the factory."

"What does he think happened?" I asked, growing a little worried.

"Why do you think he asked you to come?"

I shrugged. "I don't know. He didn't really say. He implied that because I was the owner, I needed to answer a few questions."

"He wants to pry."

"Pry into what, Mom? What has got you so worried?"

She sighed, more in resignation than frustration. "Oh, Violet. You have so much to learn."

# CHAPTER 3

*M*y mother left after getting a phone call, leaving me in the house alone to ponder her rather cryptic message. Well, not alone I guess, since according to her, Grandma's spirit was hanging out with me.

When my phone rang, I yelped and jumped about three feet in the air. All the talk about witches and ghosts had left me a little freaked out, even if I didn't actually believe in that stuff.

"Hello?" I answered.

"Violet Broussard?"

"Yes. May I ask who's calling?"

"This is Sheriff Smith. I'm sorry I missed you earlier. Do you have time to meet me at my office now, or would you like to wait until tomorrow?"

I checked my watch. It was only five, not too late at all. "I'll be right over. Give me about fifteen minutes."

After I quickly freshened up in the bathroom, I left the house. When I pulled up to the sheriff's office, he was outside waiting for me. I took in the sight of the portly, balding man—his appearance had changed very little over the past twenty years. He had aged some and lost more hair, but he still had that bumbling look about him.

"We'll drive over in my rig," he said by way of greeting.

"Drive over?" I asked, caught a little off-guard.

"To the factory."

"Oh, I didn't know I needed to go there," I said, a little uneasy about a visit to the site of a death, whether it was accidental or intentional.

He eyed me suspiciously, making me a little uncomfortable. The man had been the county sheriff forever, it seemed. I had been lucky enough to never have any real run-ins with him, but he still had a way of making me feel as if I had done something wrong.

"You can ride in the front," he said, as he motioned to his extended cab truck with the telltale wide green stripe down the side.

"Uh, thanks," I mumbled. As if I was going to ride in the back! I wasn't a criminal. I was there merely as a courtesy to him.

He drove to the factory in complete silence, and the tension in the vehicle had me on edge. It was worse than any interrogation room. Well, I assumed so anyway, considering I'd never actually been interrogated, but I imagined it was something like this.

He stopped the truck in front of the side entrance of the old building. I jumped out of the truck, anxious to get out of the small space.

"You got the key?" he asked.

"Uh, why would I? You've been in and out of here already, haven't you?" I asked, motioning to the crime tape across the door.

He smiled and nodded. "That's true. I put my own padlock on here to keep people out. Folks are curious about this place."

Once again, I had to stop myself from saying what was on my mind. He couldn't possibly believe I had anything to do with the man's death. I had been two hundred miles away.

He unlocked the padlock and pushed open the massive steel door. Light shone in from the tall windows, providing ample light to see inside on the upper floors.

"What are we doing here?" I asked, tired of the games.

"I wanted to talk to you."

The man was making me nervous. Was it really the best idea to come out here, all alone with a man I barely knew? Sure, he was the law, but that didn't mean much.

"About what? Why couldn't we talk in your office?" I asked, tamping down my growing fear.

I took a few steps to the left, suddenly not wanting to be within reach of the man.

My rubber-soled shoes were silent on the concrete floor of the factory. I took a brief second to look around, seeking escape routes, just in case. I saw plenty of potential weapons I could use if needed. All the old machines and various tools used to box up the lemon teas once produced here were all in their original places. It was eerie, as if the typical work day had ended and everyone went home, intending to return, yet never did.

The dust was thick and as we walked, it stirred up the debris on the floor. The sun streaming in through the bank of windows highlighted every little dust particle in the air.

"The man killed here was named Dale Johnson. He was one of those supernatural investigators," he explained.

I nodded my head. "Okay."

"Dale and his buddy George Cannon had been in town for about two weeks."

"Why?"

He looked at me. I could feel him sizing me up, trying to determine whether I was lying or telling the truth.

"To investigate the coven."

I felt my blood run cold. I gulped down the lump in my throat. "Coven?" I squeaked out.

"Yep, can you believe that nonsense? These guys are part of some paranormal investigator group or something like that. They travel around the country and investigate the supernatural. Dale was from Lemon Bliss and said he'd always wanted to investigate this old factory. He was convinced it was haunted and built on old witch grounds," he said, shaking his head in disbelief.

"I'm not sure what all this has to do with me, Sheriff?"

"Well, this is your property. I figured you might have an idea why these two yahoos thought there was something to find in here."

I shook my head. "I don't. I had no idea they were investigating. I mean, this is private property. Weren't they trespassing?"

He shrugged. "Well, considering one of them is dead, I don't think that's a big problem, do you? I think what we need to focus on is how a man ended up dead in your building," he said with a slightly accusing tone.

"I don't see how it's my problem at all. If I can't press charges for trespassing and I don't live around here, why is this something I need to be involved in?"

"Want to tell me who else has access to this property?"

I shrugged, "Apparently, anybody. I have keys, and my mother has a set, but considering these men got in here, I guess a locked door isn't a big deal."

"You and your mom have keys?"

I nodded, not thinking anything of the question. Of course, we had keys.

We walked across the factory floor to the metal staircase. The sheriff started to climb the stairs. When I didn't follow, he looked down at me. "This way, please."

I reluctantly took a step up and followed him to the

second floor of the four-story building. The second floor looked down over the first with more equipment on this level.

"Over here," he gestured.

I followed him to the spot he was standing and looked around. "What?"

"That George fellow told me this is where they detected some paranormal activity."

"Am I supposed to feel something?" I asked dryly.

"Well, I don't suppose you would, but thought you should know this is where the man died."

I stepped back, immediately wanting to put some distance between myself and the area. It was creepy. Maybe not supernatural creepy, but very eerie.

"Okay, now I know. I have no answers for you, not that you've really asked me any questions," I pointed out.

He stared at what looked like a laundry chute. Why there would be a laundry chute in a factory I mused.

"Helllooo!" a voice rang out below.

Sheriff Smith looked at me with frustration. I knew he recognized the voice. I certainly did, considering it had only been a few hours since I had talked to her last.

"Lila, what are you doing here?" he shouted.

I followed him back down the industrial stairs, very glad we didn't have to go to the top.

"I saw your car out front," she yelled back.

We descended the stairs to find Lila standing there.

"Oh, Violet, you're here too," she said, in that high-pitched voice.

"Hi, Lila."

"Why are you here?" he asked again.

"Harold, don't shout at me," she scolded. "I wanted to see what you found. Anything interesting?"

"Lila, you know I can't share details of an ongoing investigation."

That seemed to make her nervous. "Really? There is an investigation? What do you think happened? I heard the man was one of those supernatural investigators."

"That's the story."

"Did they find anything? I mean, was there anything supernatural?" she prodded.

Harold looked down at his feet, shuffling nervously.

"Did they?" I asked.

He shrugged. "I don't honestly know. I don't really believe in that stuff."

Lila smiled. "Well I don't think you have to believe something for it to be real."

He looked at her as if she was crazy. "That's the craziest thing I ever heard, Lila."

"I think it's only fair that we should know if we have ghosts among us. Don't you, Violet?"

I had no idea what to say. I wasn't so sure I wanted to know if there were ghosts among us. I studied Lila. Something was off. She was lying. Lila wasn't afraid of ghosts. She was one of my mother's best friends and everyone knew my mother had a very fond appreciation for the spirit world. Lila looked anxious.

Harold looked back and forth between Lila and me before throwing his hands up in the air. "Violet, I'd appreciate you sticking around for a couple days while we get this all sorted out."

"Sheriff," I started to protest, but was interrupted by Lila.

"Your mother will be thrilled to hear that," she said with a huge smile on her face.

"Why?" I glared at the law enforcement officer who wouldn't meet my eyes.

He cleared his throat. "There's something going on here, and I have a gut feeling you are involved."

"What?" I asked, horrified. "Are you crazy!"

Lila smiled and patted my arm. "Don't worry, sweetie, it will all work out. Harold is only being cautious."

The man refused to meet my eyes. I'm sure he could have felt my anger radiating off me. I was furious.

"Lila, can you give me a ride?" I asked, staring at Harold until he finally looked at me. "Is that okay or am I under arrest or something?"

"No, you're not. I'll be in touch," he promised.

Lila and I walked out of the factory. Her little green Volkswagen Beetle was parked next to the sheriff's truck.

"What was that all about?" I asked once we were on our way back to my car.

"What, dear?" Lila asked innocently.

"Why did you come out to the factory and what do you know about the man that was killed?"

"I don't know anything, dear. I was only curious," she said, in that sing-song voice of hers.

I didn't believe her. "You don't go out to an active crime scene because you are curious, Lila."

She lifted one of her dainty shoulders. "You know how I like to keep up with what happens around here."

I let it drop, but something felt off. As soon as Lila dropped me off at my car, I called Tara.

"Hi," I said, frustration evident in my voice.

"You're not coming back tomorrow are you?"

"No. Hopefully, the following day. Things are a little confusing here."

"Uh oh, that doesn't sound good."

I sighed. "No, not really. I really don't know what I can do, but it's probably best that I'm here."

"I can handle the bakery. Don't worry about it. Spend some time with your mom. Think of this as a weekend away. I hear normal people do that," she joked.

I groaned at her attempt at humor. "Thank you. I'll call

you tomorrow and let you know what's going on. Hopefully, this will all be taken care of by then."

Once back at my grandmother's house, I gave myself a little tour, walking through each room and reminiscing. When I pushed open the door to her room, it took my breath away. Her big four-poster bed was right where it always had been.

"Oh Grams," I whispered, as I walked into the room, towards her large dresser with her various bottles on the top.

Everything looked just the way she left it. I missed her dearly. A cold breeze brushed across my neck. I spun around, feeling as if someone was behind me. There was no one there. I shook off the feeling and headed back downstairs to pop in one of the microwave dinners my mom had brought me earlier.

# CHAPTER 4

$\mathcal{I}$ spent the better half of the morning, roaming through the big house. I had called Tara to check on business and was assured it was a typical Wednesday, slow and boring. We chatted for a few minutes before she had to go. Then I was left all alone in the big house.

Wide awake, I had nothing to do. No matter how hard I had tried, I hadn't been able to sleep in. I was a baker. Bakers rose with the sun. I had owned my own bakery for five years and had an internal alarm clock with no snooze button.

I quickly grew tired of the boredom and decided to go grab a cup of coffee at the coffee shop. Hungry and in need of real caffeine, I needed something stronger than the tea my mom had put in my little care package.

When I walked into Crooked Coffee, I was relieved to see it was empty, so I could enjoy my coffee in peace. I ordered a muffin as well. I always liked to check out the competition, even if this little shop wasn't really competition for my own bakery several hours away.

I sipped my coffee and took a bite of the muffin. It was

good, really good. The door opened and I looked up just in time to see Lila come through the door. *Crap.*

"Violet! There you are! I just went by the house looking for you. Coral, she's here," the woman yelled out the door.

I waited, wondering just what was going on. Why would they be looking for me?

"What's the matter?" I asked, almost dreading to find out why they needed me so badly.

Lila plopped down. "It's your mom."

I was instantly on alert. "What about my mom?"

Coral waved at me with her fingers and pulled another chair up to my tiny table.

"Hi, Violet. It's so good to see you. You look gorgeous, so much like your mama."

I anxiously nodded. "Thank you, but what's wrong with my mom?"

"Oh, nothing's *wrong* with her," Lila clarified. "It's what may happen."

I closed my eyes and counted to three. "What may happen?"

Coral and Lila exchanged a look, before Coral answered. "She's talking to Harold, and he isn't being too kind."

Lila guffawed. "Too kind? The man is like a dog with a bone. He just won't let it go."

"Why is he talking to Mom, and what won't he let go of?"

Coral cleared her throat. "Maybe we can go back to your place and talk about this?" she asked, looking around the empty shop as if she was worried we were being watched.

"Oh, Coral, nobody's listening. You're so paranoid," Lila countered.

Coral smoothed her perfectly coifed blonde hair with one hand. "I'm not paranoid. I'm careful. You should try it sometime. It would probably keep us out of this kind of trouble!" she hissed through the tight smile plastered on her face.

"Fine. Grandma's house. Let's go," I jumped up, pushing the chair back so fast it hit the back of the chair behind it.

"What a splendid idea," Coral said. "I'll grab a couple of coffees and be right there," she said, clacking across the floor in her heels.

Thankfully, it was only a five-minute drive to the house, so I didn't have to wait too long to find out what was happening. I waited on the front porch for Lila and Coral, who were apparently taking their own sweet time. I wasn't surprised they were together. My mother and her friends were always together. The only one we were missing was Magnolia, and I half-expected her to be waiting for me at the house.

When the women finally pulled up in front of the house, I was a little anxious. My mom and I weren't exactly close, but I still loved her and worried about her.

Coral carefully walked up the stairs to the porch in her heels. The color looked to be a perfect match to her purple pantsuit. The woman was always meticulously dressed and a true southern belle. I knew it to be a carefully cultivated image and had never questioned why she was insistent on presenting herself to the world like that.

"Please tell me what's going on," I said, not giving them time to start bickering about anything. I'd been around these women my entire life, and they were more like aunts than friends. They were also more like sisters than friends to each other, and as such, bickered constantly.

Lila sat down and patted my knee. "Harold has it in his head that your mom knows something about that man dying in the factory."

"Why would my mom know anything?"

Coral and Lila exchanged a look. I waited, impatient for the story.

Smoothing her hair once again, Coral finally cleared her throat. "Your mother has access to the factory."

I nodded, "And?"

"Harold is convinced she knows more than she is saying. He spoke with her before you showed up and we thought it was over, but he called her in again this morning."

"Why?"

"Well, your mother didn't exactly hide her irritation over the fact that those men were sniffing around Lemon Bliss," Lila said.

"The supernatural hunters or investigators or whatever?" I asked, struggling to follow along with the conversation. The women could really use a lesson in how to carry on a conversation with clarity.

Coral and Lila nodded. "Yes," they said in unison.

I stared at them, waiting for them to explain. Gosh, it was like pulling teeth to get real information from them. Lila ran her mouth about anyone and everything all day, every day, but now, when I actually wanted to hear what she knew, she clammed up on me.

"Okay, let me sum this up and then hopefully one of you can fill in the blanks for me, because right now I am very confused. So, some supernatural investigators have been in town investigating," I paused. "What were they investigating? I think Harold told me a coven. Is that true?"

The women exchanged a look before Coral nodded her head. "Yes."

"Okay, so they were here looking into a coven and my mom didn't like it. They somehow ended up at the factory, which my mom has access to. One dies and Harold thinks my mother did it. Is that the story?" I asked, frustration making me very cranky.

"Yes!" they both said, excitedly.

"Why does Harold think my mother would actually hurt a person for investigating a coven that isn't even real?" I refused to believe what Lila had mentioned the day before. I knew it was nonsense.

They both shrugged their shoulders. It was Coral that finally answered. "We couldn't truly say, which is why we are concerned. Did he mention anything about evidence to you?"

"No. Nothing at all, but we didn't have a chance to talk much before Lila showed up," I said, not even bothering to keep the annoyance out of my tone.

Coral turned to Lila, "You went out there?" she hissed.

"I wanted to see what he was looking for or if he found anything," she said, in a shushed voice.

"Do I need to worry that my mother is in some kind of real trouble?" I asked, heading off what was sure to be another spate of bickering between the two.

Neither of them answered me right away, which told me everything I needed to know.

"I guess I should go down to the sheriff's office. Maybe I should see about getting my mother a lawyer," I said out loud, but more to myself.

"Oh dear!" Lila exclaimed. "I don't think it's that serious."

"It's not? Isn't that why you're here?" I shot back.

Coral's lips were set in a grim line, and Lila looked shocked and very worried. I stood up, ready to leave, just as my mother's electric Prius pulled up.

"Virginia!" Lila and Coral said in unison.

I looked at them and seriously wondered if the two shared a brain. There was a very strange connection between the two of them. It was like they could read one another's thoughts.

The three of us stood there and watched as my mother got out of her car. Her long purple skirt flowed behind her as her charm bracelets tinkled with her movement.

"Hello, ladies," she greeted us with a friendly smile. "I didn't expect to find you all here."

"We were worried about you," Coral explained.

"Oh, there's nothing to worry about," my mom said,

waving a hand through the air. The top she was wearing reminded me of something from the seventies. It was probably one of my grandmother's old shirts I decided, taking in the purple and green paisley print with silver thread outlining the patterns.

"I'm fine," she said, stepping onto the porch. "I could use some water, though."

I unlocked the front door and headed inside to do her bidding. When I came back, the three women were huddled together, talking in low voices. It was evident that they were upset about something.

"What's going on?" I asked, handing my mother the water.

"Oh nothing, dear. I was just telling the girls about Harold and his silly questions," my mom answered, waving a bejeweled hand through the air.

I had never known my mother not to wear jewelry. It all looked like costume jewelry to me, but she insisted on wearing gobs of rings, charm bracelets and clunky necklaces all the time, even when we were at home. It was how I'd always known her and I didn't question it now.

"Why does Harold—Sheriff Smith—think you know something about that man's death?" I asked, not interested in beating around the bush.

She shrugged one of her dainty shoulders. "He's only doing his job."

"The girls told me you were upset about the man researching a coven. Why would that bother you?"

She looked at her friends and then at me. "We don't need unwanted attention. Lemon Bliss is a small town. We like to keep our business to ourselves."

"Who exactly is *we*?" I asked.

Once again, Lila and Coral looked uncomfortable.

"Why, all of us my dear," my mother answered, as if it was obvious.

I sat down in one of the chairs on the porch, my mother sat in my grandmother's rocking chair while Lila and Coral sat side by side on the porch swing. "Why would a supernatural investigator be interested in Lemon Bliss, Louisiana?"

Lila smiled. Coral looked as if she was hoping the earth would swallow her up, and my mother looked far too serious.

"Rumors, I suppose. According to Harold, the surviving investigator claimed to be chasing some leads, which are really nothing more than exaggerated tales," my mother explained.

"What kind of rumors? Obviously, they held enough weight for these men to come out here."

My mother smiled. "It's all really just a bunch of nonsense. If your grandmother were here, she could explain it all so much better. A long time ago, there were rumors about a group of witches living in Lemon Bliss. The witches were blamed for some of the strange happenings around town. You know how rumors are, sometimes they live forever based on nothing."

My gaze focused on Lila. She nervously squirmed on the bench seat of the swing.

"Mom, why did Lila tell me she was a witch and ask me when I was going to join the coven?"

Coral gasped. My mother's head practically spun around as she stared at Lila, whose mouth opened and closed like a fish, with no words coming out.

# CHAPTER 5

$\mathcal{I}$ waited for my mother to answer me, as Coral was shooting daggers at Lila with her eyes. I had managed to make all the women speechless which had to be some kind of first.

"Violet, I'm not sure why Lila said that," my mother said, looking at her friend before looking back at me. "However, she did say it and I think it's time we had a talk. Ladies, would you excuse us please?" she said, standing and opening the front door.

I stood and followed her into the house. I could hear Coral laying into Lila before the door closed behind me. Lila was in trouble. I felt a little bad for causing her this difficulty, but if she hadn't wanted me to repeat that little tidbit of information, she shouldn't have mentioned it.

"Sit, please," my mom ordered, taking a seat in one of the antique armchairs.

I sat on the sofa, facing her. Outside, through the large window facing the porch, I could see Lila and Coral in a heated discussion. I turned my attention to my mother and could see she was struggling.

"Just tell me," I encouraged.

She took a deep breath. "Your grandmother was a very special woman, as was her mother and so on."

I nodded my head, but didn't say anything. It wasn't anything I hadn't heard before.

"She *was* a witch. Not in the way that is often portrayed in the books and fairytales. She was a practicing witch with an affinity for spells. They were powerful, *good* witches," she stressed.

"Mom," I started to interrupt.

She held up a hand. "I'm a witch as well. It is an inherited trait that has been passed down to the women in our family for many, many generations."

"What?" I asked, blinking my eyes and feeling a little stunned.

"Your grandmother was the head of our local coven. Well, she became the head when the other family gave up their rights, but that's a story for another time," she waved her hand in the air. "When I became of age, I took my place as the head of the coven."

"Wait, you're telling me you're a witch, and part of a coven? The head of the coven?" I repeated, struggling to wrap my head around the information.

"Yes. You are a witch too, Violet. It's your birthright. We come from a long line of witches," she said, softly. "I should clarify, we are practicing witches. I don't know how much you know about witchcraft, but I imagine most of what you think you know is entirely false."

I leaned back on the couch, letting her words sink in. "I don't understand."

"You're a witch sweetie. You have abilities the average person doesn't have," she said, as if that were a good thing. I might add she didn't seem the least bit fazed by this wacky conversation. I was a *witch*?

"So, how come I've never noticed these abilities?" I asked, using air quotes around the word.

"Because you've never been taught how to use them," she said, exasperation in her voice.

I grinned. "So, you're saying I can't wiggle my nose or blink to make something appear?" I teased.

"That's just rude. You've obviously watched too much TV. This is serious and very real. I'm trying to tell you something important here. Will you please try and keep an open mind?"

I rolled my eyes. "I guess, but I don't see how I could have lived twenty-four years and never known about this. I mean, wouldn't I have seen magic? Grandma didn't have a big black cauldron and I don't remember seeing one in our kitchen, either," I quipped.

"Oh Violet, come on, this is serious. Please, try and listen to what I'm telling you."

"Fine. I won't say another word."

She let out a long breath. "A while back, things got a little dangerous. We had to hide who we were in order to protect ourselves and our families. It was before you were born. I will admit we were a little reckless back then," she said, shaking her head. "We nearly exposed ourselves."

"Who was reckless? What happened?"

She smiled, "We were just learning about our magic. We were young and careless, and I guess you could say we experimented more than we should have. A few spells back-fired and people in town started to suspect something was amiss. Your grandmother, as the head of the coven, ordered us to hide our secret at all cost."

"Who? You keep saying we."

Another wistful smiled. "The girls and I. Lila, Coral, Magnolia, and a few others," she winked.

"Why are you just now telling me this?" I asked. "I mean,

this seems like it's a really big deal. How did I never hear any of this before?"

"Well, you did hear about the stories, but by the time you were old enough, they were twisted so bad, no one but a handful of people knew who we were." She grinned, "But it's time you knew the truth. You need to know who you are. I've let you live your life without the burden of knowing our family secret. Now it's time for you to know."

"Mom, I don't even know if I believe in that stuff. It seems like urban legends and the result of some very vivid imaginations."

"You don't have to believe it, but it's true regardless of what you think."

My mind raced, thinking back to my childhood and the various stories I had heard. Back then, some of the kids had said things about me being a witch like my mom, but I ignored it. I had just chalked it up to things kids say. I remembered asking her why people said that, but she'd always blamed it on silly gossip.

"The tree," I blurted out. "The crooked oak, was that really Grandma?" I asked, remembering one of the stories I had heard throughout my childhood.

My mom chuckled. "No, that was your great-grand-mother. She did that when she was just a girl learning how to use her magic. Oh, what a hoot that would have been to see!" she slapped her thigh. "According to her, she was trying to cast a spell to make it rain. The farmers were struggling in one of the worst droughts to hit the area. Her daddy, being a farmer and knowing the truth about his wife and daughter, begged them to do something. Your great-great-grandmother refused, citing the rules of witchcraft, but your great-grandma Prudence was not one to follow the rules."

I raised my eyebrow at the ridiculous story, but listened intently. "Go on," I encouraged.

"Grandma Prudence used to tell me the story all the time," she said, with a wistful look in her eye. "She tried to create a rainstorm to help her daddy, and she was successful, but the rain came with a violent thunderstorm. A bolt of lightning struck that giant oak. So, the locals have the story half-right. It was hit by lightning, but the lightning was the result of a spell gone wrong."

I thought about some of the other rumors and what were considered local urban legends. "What about Coral hexing that girl? The one that was flirting with her boyfriend?"

My mother shook her head. "Yes, that one is also true. Coral let jealousy rule and nearly exposed us all. Thankfully, my mom and some of the other ladies in the coven managed to create enough doubt in the minds of the people in town that it was brushed aside as a silly rumor."

"What did she do?" I asked, finding myself intrigued.

"I shouldn't tell you, but she gave the girl the most horrible case of acne you ever did see."

I fought back a giggle. "That's kind of funny."

"No, not at all. We never use our magic for personal gain. Coral learned a very hard lesson. It was that spell and a few others from times gone by that caused the coven to have to hide. We could no longer take such risks. That's why Coral is the way she is today. She faced a great deal of scrutiny back then and her boyfriend ended up breaking up with her anyway because he was afraid of her," she explained.

"Oh," I said, understanding why Coral went to such great lengths to look and act normal. My mother was the opposite. She dressed the part. Lila had dyed her hair lavender with silver streaks through it. Magnolia always wore what she referred to as her talisman, a massive silver necklace, and had several black cats. They embraced some of the witch stereotypes, while Coral avoided all of it, choosing instead to be the picture of current fashion.

"I hope you understand and will accept your destiny," my mom said softly.

"What are you talking about? I don't have to accept anything. Mom, I'm sorry, but I don't believe in witchcraft and spells and all that stuff."

"Violet Broussard! You come from a long line of proud witches. You cannot deny your heritage!"

"Uh, actually I can. Especially if I think it's a bunch of silly nonsense, which I do. I appreciate the stories, but you have to admit, they can all be explained another way. There is no factual evidence to back up your claims," I told her, not buying her story for a minute.

"Look around you, Violet. Look at the flowers outside. That is your grandmother's handiwork. You don't always have to see to believe," she said, and I could hear the hurt in her voice.

"Mom, I can appreciate that you believe you are a witch, and if Lila and Coral believe they are witches, that's fine, too. But I don't," I said, as gently as possible.

She was shaking her head. "This is my fault," she mumbled. "I should have told you sooner, but I knew it would be difficult for you. Your grandmother wanted to tell you when you were eleven, but I refused."

"If you truly believe you are a witch and you actually believed I inherited some magical qualities, why wouldn't you tell me? Why would you come up with this story today? A day you are being questioned about the death of a man? Mom, are you trying to cover something up?" I asked, suddenly very worried.

"No! It isn't like that. Our secret must be guarded at all costs," she shot back, standing as she began to pace the room."

"At all costs? That sounds ominous."

"Oh, stop it. I told you the truth. We have to stick together, Violet."

That made me angry. "How can we stick together if you've been hiding this deep, dark secret from me?" I asked, my voice rising and my patience wearing thin.

The sound of the door closing drew both our attention. It was Lila.

"Dear, you have to try and understand why your mom did what she did," Lila was saying softly, walking towards me.

"No, I don't. Don't feed into her crazy ramblings," I grumbled.

"Oh, sweetie, it's not crazy. It's true. Long ago, we all decided it was best we kept our secret to ourselves to protect the next generation."

I shook my head. I'd had enough. I was not going to stand there and listen to them try to tell me I was a witch, they were witches and there was a secret coven. It was then a thought occurred to me. My stomach dropped as I followed the train of thought before turning to my mother to look directly into her eyes.

"You said you had to protect the coven at all cost. The man who died was investigating the coven, and the rumors that were attributed to it," I said, my voice suddenly hoarse.

"Yes."

I could feel the blood rushing from my face. "What did you do?" I whispered.

Lila and my mother looked at each other. Neither of them spoke. I couldn't be in the same room with them another minute. I had to get away. I needed time to process everything.

"I'm leaving," I stormed out the door, letting the screen slam shut behind me.

# CHAPTER 6

y head was spinning with information. My mother had always been a little, ahem, quirky, but this was beyond quirky. I wondered if she could be suffering from some kind of dementia. She wasn't even fifty, but I supposed it was called early onset for a reason. I drove down Crooked Street, not really having any place to actually go.

I found myself pulling up in front of the coffee shop for the second time that day. It was the only place there was to go. I walked in, ordered another coffee and plopped down at one of the few tables, hoping to hide from the world while I tried to absorb the crazy news that I was allegedly a witch. Right.

I pulled out my phone and checked my email, anything to distract my brain from the larger topic that seemed to be trying to hog up all the brainwaves. I didn't want to think about witches and magic. That stuff wasn't real. It was make believe.

"Hey, there," a deep male voice said, interrupting my perusal of email.

I looked up to see Gabriel standing there, a cup of coffee in his hand. "Hi," I said.

"Can I join you?" he asked, gesturing to the empty chair across from me.

I looked around the empty shop and shrugged a shoulder. "Sure. I don't know if I'm very good company, though."

"Uh oh, did the sheriff give you a hard time?" he asked, with a small grin.

"I wish. He would be easier to deal with."

"Ah, I know that look. Family. Family always has a way of putting that look on your face," he smiled, leaning back in his chair.

I chuckled. "There's a reason I moved away."

"And here I moved here on purpose to be closer to mine."

"Coral's your aunt?" I asked, thinking back to what my mother had said. If Coral was a witch, that would mean Gabriel's mother was likely a witch. Oh my God! What was I thinking? I was actually buying into this ridiculous story.

"Yes, she is. My mother is her younger sister," he explained.

I nodded. "Does your mother live here as well? I don't think I remember her."

The smile on his face was sweet, but sad. "No, she passed away a few years back. We lived in New Orleans. I moved back here to get away from that scene and to be closer to Coral and my mom's roots. I wanted a fresh start."

"Oh, I'm sorry. Here I am complaining about my mother and well, I guess you would probably like to complain about yours," I said, feeling horrible for my earlier comments.

He grinned. "Trust me, when mom was alive, I complained about her as well. I think that's what mothers are supposed to do. They make you crazy. I know your mother and I really like her. She is a bit eccentric, but I love how calm she is. She always seems so at peace with herself

44

and just has this way of making me feel at ease. Just kind of ebbing and flowing and doing as she pleases."

I started to giggle at his description of her. "That is a different way to describe her. I guess I never thought of her like that, but you're right, that sums her up perfectly."

"She's a good lady. I like her," he reiterated.

I sipped my coffee, feeling a little guilty for being so frustrated with my mother. What she believed was her business.

"Why a fresh start?" I asked, mulling over what he had said.

The look on his face told me I had pried.

"I'm sorry. I shouldn't have asked that," I said, instantly feeling guilty for overstepping.

"No, it's fine. I needed a fresh start once mom passed away. There was nothing for me there, but some bad memories. Originally, I wanted to move out to California, but Aunt Coral insisted I come here and stay with her for a bit to see if I could find my way again, as she called it."

I nodded my head, pretending to understand, but not really getting it. "I'm sorry, that must have been very difficult for you. Were you and your mom close?"

He smirked. "I don't know if you could say that. We had some struggles. It's a long, sordid story, probably not the best for a coffee date."

I chuckled. "Is this a coffee date? I thought it was more of a running into each other kind of date."

That seemed to ease the tension that had fallen over us after the mom bomb.

"Slow work day?" I asked, trying to think of something else to talk about besides my mother or his.

"Lunch break."

I nodded, trying to think of something else to say, but didn't get the chance. Coral breezed into the shop, spotted us in the corner and headed our way. Her purple heels clacked and echoed across the room as she sauntered towards us as if she were on a Paris runway.

She snatched a chair from an empty table and dragged it to ours before plopping down.

"Hi, Coral, have a seat," I said dryly.

Gabriel raised an eyebrow before turning to his aunt. "What's up, Aunt Coral?"

She released an exaggerated sigh before reaching out and covering my free hand with both of hers. "Oh, honey, I heard about what happened. Are you okay?" she asked with real concern.

"What happened?" Gabriel asked looking at me with the same unnecessary concern.

"Nothing happened. My mother and I had a disagreement. How did you hear? I thought you left?" I asked. She had been gone when I left the house.

Coral was shaking her head and making weird sounds. "Such an awful thing. I'm sorry. Things just seem to be spiraling out of control. I wish things could have been different."

I looked at her as if she were crazy. I was beginning to think she was. I didn't know how much Gabriel knew, so I chose my words carefully. "It's all fine. I'm not worried about it."

She cocked her head to the side and studied me carefully. "You're not?"

"No. I'm only here for today. My mother can do what she wants and believe whatever makes her happy."

Coral nodded her head and patted my hand. "That's true. One day, I hope the two of you can believe together. Right now, we need to worry about getting this other business handled."

Gabriel was looking at us strangely. "Are you sure everything is okay? What business?"

I ignored his last question. "Yes, everything is fine," I said firmly. "My mom, Coral and Lila seem to have some strange idea about me moving back here. I guess they don't understand I moved away and started a new life. A life I am quite happy with," I said, looking pointedly at Coral.

She stared at me for several long seconds. My stomach twisted. I prayed she wouldn't reveal the family secret, or at least what my mother called the family secret. Gabriel seemed like a nice guy and I didn't want him to think we were all crazy.

"Gabriel, dear, are you busy this afternoon?" she said, turning away from me.

He shook his head. "Nope, just finishing a job at Mrs. Blankenship's and then I'm free. What do you need?"

The woman plastered on a brilliant smile. "Great! You can keep Violet busy while she waits for Harold to figure out what he wants to do with her."

I nearly choked on the hot liquid in my mouth. "Excuse me?" I croaked out.

"Gabriel is free this afternoon. You're free, why not have dinner together? You can drive over to Ruby Red and spend a quiet evening alone," she explained, referring to a neighboring town. "That way, you won't have to worry about any of us nosey old ladies bothering you."

Oh, Coral was good. Very smooth. She had managed to set us up, right in front of us, without either one of us having any idea what she was doing.

I cleared my throat. "Coral, I'm sure Gabriel has better things to do."

"Actually, I don't," he said with a sly grin on his face.

"Lovely!" Coral clapped her hands together. "You can keep Violet busy. I would hate for her visit home to be soured by a tiny little argument with her mother. You show her a good time and convince her to stick around," she said, winking at her nephew.

I stared, mouth agape as the woman went about planning my life with an all-too-willing co-conspirator. "Um, I'm not staying. Actually, I'm going to head over to the sheriff's office to see if he really needs me."

Coral got very serious. "He might not need you, but we do." Her gaze held mine. I couldn't look away.

I involuntarily leaned back in my chair. Her tone and the expression on her face intimidated me. The woman was always so sunny and bubbly. This was a different side of Coral. One I had never seen before. I didn't think I wanted to see it again.

"I will likely stay today since it's already past lunch and I don't want to drive home in the dark, not on these winding roads," I explained, hoping to placate her.

As if she had been briefly possessed, her typical exterior appeared again and she was all smiles. "That's lovely dear. You two have a good time. I'll leave you alone, now," she said, standing and putting her chair back before breezing out of the coffee shop as if she'd never been there.

It was then I realized she hadn't even ordered anything. How did she know where to find me? I shook it off, assuming she must have known where Gabriel was. It was a little eerie to feel as if I was being constantly watched and monitored.

"I'm really sorry about that," Gabriel said.

"It's fine," I mumbled, still trying to recover from the Coral whirlwind.

"She can be a bit of a spitfire," he joked.

"Ya, she sure can. If you're busy, please don't feel obligated," I said, secretly hoping he would back out.

"I would like to take you out, that is if you still want to."

I thought about it for a second and threw caution to the wind. "Sure, I'd like that."

He grinned. "Can I pick you up at six?"

"Yes, I would like that very much."

"Perfect, I'll be there."

I took a sip of coffee. "Gabriel, uh, I didn't bring anything fancy to wear."

"Good, because I don't do fancy. I prefer casual and comfortable," he replied nonchalantly.

We each drank our coffee in silence for a few more minutes. I was still mortified by Coral's actions. I couldn't believe she foisted me on her nephew. I was going to have to talk to my mom about her friends trying to set me up. It was not okay.

"I should go. I need to track down the sheriff," I said, standing to leave.

"Yep, me too. I'll see you tonight."

I smiled at him and left the shop. To think I had been bored earlier in the day. This had quickly turned into one of the strangest days of my life and the day was only half over. I couldn't imagine what the evening held. I shook off the feeling of foreboding and headed to the sheriff's office, hoping to catch him. The sooner I got this whole mess sorted out, the sooner I could go home and forget all about witches and magic spells.

# CHAPTER 7

*M*y hopes of resolving the situation with the sheriff were immediately dashed when I discovered he would be spending time in a neighboring town. As I drove back to my grandma's house, I thought about everything my mother had said. It was too crazy to believe. The practical side of me wanted to dismiss it all, but there was another part of me that accepted it as the truth. I didn't even know what to think about *that*. Every time the thought that it felt true passed through my mind, I swatted it away and reminded myself that was plain crazy.

I wasn't prepared to spend another night in town and would need to pick up a few things. The small market with inflated prices was my only option. I pulled in, but before getting out of my car, I looked around. Lila and Coral always seemed to appear out of nowhere. I wasn't prepared to see either of them. Not now. Not when I was still trying to make heads or tails of my mother's revelations.

I grabbed a basket and began to browse the aisles, looking for staples to sustain me for another day.

"Oh, there you are, honey!"

I froze. It was uncanny how these women managed to find me so quickly. It made me even more suspicious of them all.

Slowly, I turned to face Lila. "What do you need?" I asked, almost afraid to ask.

"I've been worried about you."

"Why?"

"You left in such a hurry. I just wanted you to understand that your mother wasn't trying to hurt you or make you mad," she explained.

"It's fine, Lila."

Turning back to face the numerous bags of chips before me, I was aware of someone coming down the aisle.

"Lila! What brings you here? I never see you in here," a woman's voice called out.

I turned to see who was talking. It was a familiar face, but I couldn't remember her name. She was about the same age as Lila and my mom. I studied her close, wondering if she was one of the other women in the coven my mom referred to.

Hoping to slip away, I ignored them, hoping I could ease on out without Lila noticing. I didn't get far.

"So I hear you have a date tonight with our handsome Gabriel?"

I stopped walking, took a deep breath and spun around to face her. The other woman was still there.

"Our Gabriel?" the woman repeated. "Coral's nephew?"

Lila was grinning and nodding her head. "Yes, Coral set them up earlier this afternoon."

Suddenly I wondered if maybe the town was bugged. The way information traveled at lightning speed was nothing short of a miracle.

"They are a perfect match," the unidentified woman declared.

Staring at her, I decided she had to be one of them. She

didn't look like a witch, but did I really know what a witch looked like?

"Gotta run. I'd like to shower before my dinner date tonight," I said, somewhat sarcastically.

Lila grinned. "How exciting! I hope you two have a great time, and I can't wait to hear all about it."

It was my fervent hope that she heard nothing about it. She didn't need to know every detail of my life.

A thought occurred to me. "Lila, can I have a minute?" I asked.

She turned to the other woman, said her goodbyes and then came to stand close to me. "What is it, dear?"

"Is she one?"

"One?" she asked, a confused look on her face.

I lowered my voice to a whisper, "One of the coven."

"No, no. It's just me, Coral, Magnolia, and your mother. Our numbers have dwindled. When things got a little, uh, dicey, we were forced to go underground. It's just our four families now," she said, in a decidedly wistful tone.

Nodding, I wasn't sure I believed her, but it made sense. Well, as much sense as any of this whole witch thing made.

"Okay. Well, I better get going," I said, and quickly headed down the aisle.

Tossing in a few more things, I quickly paid and managed to escape before Lila could corner me again.

Driving straight to the house, I locked the front door and headed for the shower. I regretted not having any other clothes with me. Despite how Coral had all but cornered me into this dinner date, I wanted to look good. Gabriel was handsome and charming, even tempting if I let myself admit it. I pulled the few items I had brought with me out of my small overnight bag. Slim pickings.

The doorbell rang, giving me a small heart attack. It couldn't be Gabriel. I still had a couple of hours before my date. I pulled on the shorts I had brought to sleep in and threw on my t-shirt.

The doorbell rang again. "Hold on!" I called out.

Yanking open the door, I found my mother standing there with two more bags.

"What's that?" I asked, pointing to the bags.

She smiled and breezed past me. "I brought you some clothes for your date tonight."

"What?" I said, shutting the door.

"You can't go out with a young man wearing jeans and a t-shirt. I know I taught you better than that," she lectured.

I raised my eyebrows, "Mom, I don't think we really have the same style," I said, horrified at the thought of wearing some of her flamboyant clothes.

She waved away my protest. "I brought conservative choices. You could use some spicing up."

I rolled my eyes, frustrated. "I don't need spicing up. I happen to like the way I dress. I don't need to impress anyone, anyway. I go to work and home," I said, feeling irritated I had to defend my wardrobe.

She shrugged. "And now it's time for you to spice things up. Dress up. Embrace your gorgeous figure. Gabriel is a very handsome man. Don't you want to look good for him?"

"This isn't the twentieth century anymore, Mom."

Even if I'd just been thinking I didn't want to look like a slob, I wasn't about to admit that to her.

"It doesn't hurt to put in a little effort, dear. Here, what do you think of this?" she held up a black skirt with pretty silver threads running through it.

Actually, I liked it. It wasn't too eccentric, and was something I could work with. "Fine."

"Now, I brought a couple of different options for the top. The weather is warm so I thought this sparkly tank top would bring out the shimmer in the skirt," she said, holding up the shirt in question.

I shook my head. "Nope, I don't do sparkly."

She groaned and pulled out a plain black top that had sheer, flowing sleeves. "This?"

I wrinkled my nose. "I'll look like I'm dressed for a funeral. Or like a witch," I added, just to get under her skin.

"Stop it. Witches don't wear all black. That's an old wives' tale." She reached into her bag and pulled out a lavender tank with a flowing waistline.

"That one I like," I said, taking in the subdued color.

"So plain," she commented. "I have some black sandals here that I know will match perfectly," she held up the shoes.

"Thanks, Mom."

"You're welcome. Now, go get dressed."

I grabbed the items and raced upstairs to change. I twirled around, checking out my reflection in the full-length mirror. It wasn't too bad at all.

"What do you think?" I asked, coming downstairs.

"You look beautiful. Now, I'm going to get out of here. I don't want you two to feel awkward. I'm sure Coral already did a fine job of that."

"Yes, she did. Thank you again for the clothes. I'll call you tomorrow before I leave."

"Leave?"

"Mom, I have to get back to work. I was only planning on being here for a day."

"We'll see. We need you, Violet, but we'll worry about that later. Have fun," she said, walking out the door.

Her words were a little strange. We'll see what? I wondered, but I didn't have time to ponder what she meant for long. Gabriel showed up fifteen minutes early.

"Hi," I greeted him.

He was wearing a pair of jeans, a jacket and tie. I was so glad my mom had showed up with the clothes. I would have been sorely underdressed.

"You're early," I greeted him.

He shrugged a shoulder, giving me an aw shucks look. "I don't like to be late."

"Well, I'm hungry, so it works for me."

We drove the twenty minutes to the next town and sat down at an Italian restaurant.

"I think I need to be up front with you," he started, instantly putting me on alert.

"About?"

"My aunt."

I pretended to be clueless. He could be apologizing for the set-up or any number of things. I didn't want to show my hand and say too much.

"What about your aunt?"

He cleared his throat. "I assume you know she is a..." he paused and looked around the restaurant "...a witch," he whispered.

"I recently heard that bit of information," I acknowledged.

"She and my mom both believed themselves to be witches," he explained. "I humor them. I'm not a witch or warlock or whatever the correct term is. It's a family thing, my grandma claimed to be one and so on. They didn't talk a lot about it. I guess me being a guy and all I wasn't privy to their secrets. They were open about who they were in our family, but it was never to be talked about in mixed company, as my mom would say."

"Thank you for telling me. Are there many other witches around here?" I asked, as if joking, but I was dead serious.

He grinned. "I don't know. I figured we should get that all right out in the open. Aunt Coral is usually really careful, but in case there are rumors or something, I wanted you to hear it right from the horse's mouth," he said with a disarming smile.

"Are there a lot of rumors?" I asked, excited to find another source of information.

"I don't know if you would say a lot. I've heard a little since I've been here, but nothing bad. Until the death at the factory, that is. That's got the rumor mill working overtime."

"Why?"

He studied me closely before taking a deep breath. "Your mom has been at the center of the rumors. A few people suspect she may know more than she says."

"What! Why would they think that?"

"Maybe because the sheriff keeps questioning her?" he asked, appearing to be just as puzzled.

"My mom is a lot of things, but she's definitely not a murderer," I said firmly.

He held up his hands. "Wait, I'm not saying I believe the rumors. Not at all. I like your mom."

I breathed a sigh of relief, just as the waiter came to the table. We ordered and then sat in silence for several long minutes.

"Gabriel, what are you doing tomorrow?"

He shrugged and appeared to be mulling over his schedule. "Nothing that I know of. Why?"

I leaned forward, not wanting to be overheard. "I want to go out to the factory and look around. I feel like the sheriff was trying to get me to say something or show him something, but I didn't know what. I didn't get the chance to ask because Lila showed up."

He nodded his head. "You want to do your own investigating?"

"Yes. I have the keys so we can go in a different door and never touch the crime scene tape, so I don't think it would necessarily be illegal. Besides, I own the place and I've never really been inside. I want to see if I can find out what those supernatural investigators were looking for."

His gaze narrowed. "Isn't that dangerous? I mean, the last guy that snooped around there is dead."

"That's why I want you along!"

"You want me to protect you, or you want to up your own odds of escape?"

We both laughed. "I was there with the sheriff. The only thing dangerous I saw was the amount of dust in the place."

"Okay. I'm up for a little sleuthing around."

"Great."

Our food was delivered a short time later. We dug in and our conversation switched to more normal first-date topics about our work and what music we liked.

When he pulled up in front of my house, I paused before getting out of his truck.

"Gabriel?"

"Yes?"

"Please don't tell your aunt about our plans tomorrow. I don't want anyone else to know, especially my mom or Lila."

"Got it. My lips are sealed. Good night."

# CHAPTER 8

*T*here was no way I was going home today. Somehow I knew that as sure as I knew I wanted coffee. The moment I opened my eyes, I had a weird feeling about the day. It was strange. I chalked it up to all the talk about witches and the supernatural, and the fact that I was about to sneak into the factory, the site of an active crime scene.

"Hi," I said, when Tara answered the phone.

"Hey. What's wrong?" she asked.

I sighed. "Nothing. I can't come home today. This whole thing is taking a lot longer than I thought. Are you sure everything is okay there?"

"Everything is fine. The shop is still standing, sales are still coming in. I got this, Violet," she assured me.

"Thank you, Tara. I owe you a huge bonus for taking on all the extra responsibility."

"I'm your assistant manager. This is what I'm supposed to do, you just never let me do it. It's kind of fun being the boss," she teased.

"Don't get too comfortable in my chair."

"What have you been doing down there?"

I hesitated, debating how much I wanted to tell her, but I knew she wouldn't buy the nothing line. "I went out on a date last night," I blurted out.

"Excuse me? You did what?" she squealed.

I giggled, feeling my cheeks heat even though I was alone. "I went out on a date with a very attractive, eligible man."

"How was it?"

"Fun. He's easy to talk to and isn't scared off by my eccentric mother. He likes her. He's really laid back. Oh, and did I mention he is very good looking?"

"Now I see why you don't want to come back. Tell me everything!"

We talked for a while before she had to go. I missed her, but being here in my grandma's house felt right somehow. I could feel a pull to protect my mother. It was hard to explain, but I assumed it was the mother-daughter bond.

I quickly showered and changed into one of the two outfits I'd brought with me. I was going to have to go shopping. Maybe Gabriel would want to hang out for the day, and we could go over to Ruby Red together.

What was I thinking? I was planning on spending the day with the man, doing things that were typically reserved for actual couples. I was jumping in with both feet and needed to take a step back. I was only here temporarily, I reminded myself. The last thing I needed was to get caught up in the idea of romance.

I heard the doorbell and ran downstairs.

"Hi!" I greeted Gabriel who had a look of apprehension. "What's wrong?" I asked, hoping there wasn't anything actually the matter.

"Nothing. I feel guilty. Why do I feel guilty? We haven't even done anything, yet?"

I laughed. "I do actually own the factory. I can show you the deed if it will set your mind at ease."

He shook his head. "No, that's fine. I had to lie to Coral this morning. She asked me what I was doing. I told her I was going shopping in Ruby Red."

"Actually, maybe you weren't lying."

"What do you mean?"

"I was going to ask if you had the day free if you wanted to go over there with me? I need to do some shopping. I only brought clothes for an overnight stay and really need to pick up a few things," I explained.

I had to take a step back when he turned on that charming smile once again. The man was dangerous. "I would love that. Maybe you can buy me lunch since I'm breaking the law and everything for you."

I laughed and grabbed my purse. "It isn't breaking the law. Not really, I don't think. Now, let's go before you chicken out."

He playfully glared at me before turning around and heading out the door. I didn't want to admit I was on the verge of backing out myself. My stomach was a jumble of nerves, but I had to do this. Something felt off and I needed to figure out what it was. My intuition told me my mother and her friends were involved. I didn't know to what extent, but they definitely knew more than what they were saying.

"Pull around back, so no one sees your truck," I instructed once he reached the old factory.

He parked close to the building in the back. The factory itself hid his truck from anyone driving by. No one would be able to see it unless they were driving around the back on the old dirt roads that led to a small lake. No one ever went back there. We got out of the truck and I immediately saw a collection of footprints in the dirt.

"Whoa! Look at this," I said pointing to the evidence covering the ground.

Gabriel looked down. "I thought you said this place was abandoned. It looks to me like it's been very busy."

"Maybe it was the investigators?" I offered.

He shrugged a shoulder. "Maybe. I haven't heard about any of the local kids partying out here, but that's a possibility too. Look at the footprints over there. They look kind of small to belong to a man," he pointed out.

"Yes, they do," I mumbled. "Come on, let's get this over with."

I fumbled with the key ring, trying to find the right key to fit narrow back door. I finally found it and pushed it open. We both started coughing as the dust stirred up in front of us.

"Let's go up to the second floor," I whispered.

"Why are you whispering?" he asked in a whisper.

I paused. "I don't know," I laughed.

He followed me as I crossed the first floor, weaving around the various pieces of large equipment on the floor. I made my way up the stairs.

"This is as far as I got last time I was here. Lila came in and interrupted the tour."

"What's on this floor?" he asked, looking around.

"More equipment as far as I know. The third floor is packaging stuff if I remember right, and the fourth floor is offices."

He looked around the area. "Why don't we start on the fourth floor and work our way down. What are we looking for exactly?"

"Uh, I don't actually know. Anything that seems out of place."

"Don't you think the sheriff would have already gone over all of this?"

I shrugged. "Probably, but I feel like there is something here. Something no one wants found."

He gave me a strange look, but didn't question my feeling. We went to the far end of the building and climbed the industrial stairs to the third floor. Unlike the second floor, this floor was closed in. You couldn't see to the factory floor. There were various machines and old cardboard boxes littering the area.

"Should we search the boxes?" Gabriel asked, looking at the stacks scattered around the area.

I groaned. "I don't know. Let's check the top floor first and then we'll decide. Maybe we'll find something obvious up there."

He didn't look convinced. I wasn't convinced either, but something was pulling me upstairs. I just knew I needed to look there. We ascended the last flight of stairs, both of us looking around.

"Maybe we should split up. You go left and I'll go right," I suggested.

"Is that a good idea? I mean, someone died here recently. They may have been doing the same thing."

I thought about it for a second and realized he was probably right. "Okay, let's start in here," I said, pushing open the door to the first office on my left.

"You check the desk and I'll check the bookshelf," Gabriel instructed.

I started pulling open drawers, only to be disappointed to find them empty.

"Anything?" I asked.

He shook his head. "Old paperwork and invoices, but nothing that screams ghosts and goblins were here."

I let out a long sigh. It felt futile. "Let's check the next office."

"Violet, it would really help if I knew what I was looking for."

I shrugged and shook my head. "I don't know exactly. The supernatural guys were here to investigate rumors of a coven," I said, pretending I had never heard of such a thing.

"I want to see if there is anything to the rumors. Was there anything to find?"

"Do witches and covens leave journals?" he asked.

Laughing, I continued, "I have no idea, but those guys thought they were going to find something."

I pushed away the feeling of foreboding that crept up my spine again. I knew my mother was worried, as was Lila. I needed to know if they were involved in this man's death. If so, what were they trying to hide?

"Alright, we'll keep looking."

We wandered from office to office, finding nothing that looked incriminating or even interesting. It wasn't until the last office that we found something.

"What is that stuff?" I asked, looking at what appeared to be modern electronics.

Gabriel lifted one of the small black boxes. "I don't know. Maybe a speaker or a microphone?"

I looked at it and agreed with him. We found a laptop, but the battery was dead and we couldn't find a charger.

"I'm assuming this must have been left by the investigators," I said, picking up another device that looked like something from Ghostbusters.

Gabriel nodded his head. "Check this out."

I walked to the corner where he was looking into a box. "Wow," I said, taking in the contents. It was filled with VHS tapes.

"Do you think they had cameras up?"

I immediately looked up at the ceiling. "Where?"

"Cameras could be anywhere. I wasn't looking for cameras when we came in. Maybe we should?"

"I'm going to take these with us. I want to see if there is anything recorded on these tapes."

"Aren't they evidence in a crime?" he asked, one eyebrow raised.

I shrugged a shoulder. "If the sheriff wanted them, he

could have taken them. Either he wasn't interested or he didn't find them. They were in plain sight."

Gabriel didn't look convinced, but didn't try and stop me. "I don't see anything else. This equipment has to be worth a lot of money. I wonder if the other guy will be back to collect it."

"The sheriff may not let him in."

"We're in," he pointed out.

"But the sheriff doesn't know that."

"Maybe we should get out of here. This place is giving me the creeps."

I had to agree with him. "Alright, I want to make a quick sweep of the third floor, though."

"Fine, but quick. I want to get out of here."

We walked back down the stairs and quickly checked a few of the boxes on the third floor. Most were empty while others contained old, empty lemon tea containers.

"This is good. If I find anything interesting on the tapes, we can always come back," I stated.

"Uh, or not."

I laughed. "You can't be afraid of ghosts. Your mom was a witch."

"And?"

"And by proxy, you shouldn't be afraid of ghosts. Maybe you can talk to the spirits," I teased.

"I'd rather not. Let's go."

We headed towards the back door. Gabriel stopped me from walking right out, wanting to make sure no one was waiting for us. When he declared the coast was clear, we both practically ran for the truck. Being in the factory had made us both feel very uneasy.

"Ruby Red?" he asked.

"Sure. I'm going to hide these in the backseat."

"Do you even have a VCR to watch those on?"

I smiled. "I'm sure my grandmother does. She didn't

throw anything away. I still haven't ventured up to the attic, but I can guarantee everything she has ever owned is up there somewhere."

He laughed and headed for the road that would lead us out of town. I looked in the side mirror, watching the massive factory building get smaller and smaller. There was something about that place. I didn't know what, but I hoped I would find the answer on the tapes.

# CHAPTER 9

*O*ur trip to Ruby Red ended up being another dinner date. I had really enjoyed myself. It was rather odd to hang out with a guy and go shopping, but we had a good time. Gabriel was funny and seemed to be having just as much fun as I was. By the time we got back to town, it was well past my bedtime. My typical schedule meant I was up by four in the morning, which meant I was usually in bed by nine. It was ten by the time I walked through the front door.

I touched my finger to my lips and smiled. Gabriel had been a total gentleman and walked me to the door before giving me a sweet kiss goodnight. I headed upstairs with my bags of new clothes and crawled into bed, exhausted from the busy day.

I woke up a little later than usual. The moment I opened my eyes, I sensed something was off.

*The tapes.* I had left them in Gabriel's truck.

I groaned and rolled out of bed, looking for my cell. My eyes focused on the time. It was just after five. Probably a little too early to call him. I sent him a quick text instead. Then it was downstairs for coffee.

By the time I showered and dressed in my new clothes, I was chomping at the bit to watch those videos. While I waited for Gabriel to text back, I made the climb into the attic to see if I could find a VCR. I searched for an hour with no luck.

"Dammit!"

I was going to have to hunt one down. My mother was anti-television. That was a dead end. It wasn't like there was anywhere to buy one in Lemon Bliss. Someone had to have one. I could hear my phone ringing and raced out of the attic, nearly breaking my ankle in my haste.

"Hello?" I answered, not recognizing the number.

"Is this Violet Broussard?"

"Yes. Who's this?"

"My name is George Cannon. I would like to talk to you about the lemon tea factory. Do you have some time to meet?"

I was instantly on guard. "Um, I'm sorry, but who are you?"

"George Cannon," he repeated.

I was getting frustrated and I could tell he was as well. "I'm sorry sir, but your name isn't familiar to me. How'd you get my number? And who are you?"

"I'm a supernatural investigator. I am—I was—Dale Johnson's partner. We've been investigating this area and the paranormal activity surrounding this area for the past couple of weeks."

I didn't answer.

"Dale was the man who was found dead in the factory you own. A title search revealed your name and it wasn't hard to get your number. We need to talk."

"Oh," I said. "What can I do for you?"

"I'd like to talk. Can you meet me?"

Instinct told me to be cautious. "No," I said firmly.

"I'm sorry, but I really need to talk to you. I know where you live," he added.

"Excuse me? Are you threatening me?"

"No, no, no. I simply meant I know where you live. I can meet you at your place. I'd prefer that actually."

"I don't know you, and I don't want you coming to my house. I'm not comfortable with that. What is it you need to talk to me about?"

He grumbled something under his breath. "I see. Obviously, you're protecting them," he grumbled, disdain evident in his voice.

"Protecting who? I'm not protecting anyone. I'm sorry you find it strange I don't want strangers showing up at my door."

"Dale told me about the women in this town. He grew up in Lemon Bliss and spent months researching the town and that factory. He was on to what was happening and he was going to expose everything," he seethed. "I'm not going to let you people get away with this."

The man had my guard up. "I don't know what you're talking about, but obviously you have some ideas. I can't imagine why we need to meet to talk, but I don't appreciate the way you're speaking to me. I suggest you take your complaints to the sheriff. He can help you. I can't," I said, preparing to end the call.

"My partner died!" he shouted, before I could hit the end button.

"I understand that sir and I am sorry for that, but I don't see how I can help. You need to talk with the police, not me."

"You can fill in the blanks. I *know* you know something. I want to know what he found. I want to know why he was killed. What did he find?" he shouted.

I took a deep breath. Clearly the man was grieving and I

could understand that, but I didn't see how meeting would help. I knew nothing. My mind suddenly went to the tapes. There could be a clue on the tapes.

"Mr. Cannon, I'm very sorry about your friend. However, I don't know that the sheriff has ruled it a homicide. There's still an investigation going," I said as gently as possible. "You really need to talk to him. I know nothing."

"Did you know your mother and a woman named Lila visited the factory quite often? What are they trying to hide?"

I couldn't speak. He had caught me off guard. I suspect that was his intention. He wanted me to say something that he could use. I wasn't going to give it to him.

"I don't know what you're talking about, but I guess you should probably tell the sheriff, not me," I shot back. "I can't help you. Please don't call me and don't you dare stop by. I will call the sheriff if you do either."

"Oh, I plan to talk with the sheriff. We'll see if he does anything. You people all protect one another!" he spat out. "I don't need your cooperation to run the story. I have Dale's notes and I will find his other research. If the sheriff doesn't do anything, I will take it to the state police."

"Do what you must," I said, and ended the call.

His words left me more shaken than I wanted to admit. My mom and Lila had been seen going to the factory. Why? Why would they visit an empty building? It explained why Lila had been acting weird and why the sheriff had questioned my mother, not once, but twice. My mind whirred as I went over everything he had said.

He said he was running the story. What story? Was he going to expose my mother for a witch? I groaned. It wouldn't take them long to decide I was a witch as well. What a mess.

I had to find out what was on those tapes.

It was almost eight and I still had no response from Gabriel. I was not a patient person by nature. I paced the room a few times before finally giving in. I couldn't wait any longer. I called him, assuming he'd have to be up by now. I hoped.

"Hi," he answered. "I'm glad you called."

"Hi, I'm sorry, I hope I didn't wake you."

"Nope, I was just getting ready to head out the door. What's up?"

"I sent you a text. I forgot those tapes in your truck. I was wondering if I could meet you somewhere to pick them up?"

"Oh, shoot, I forgot all about them as well. I can bring them by before I head out to my first job. Did you find a VCR?" he asked.

I sighed. "Not yet, but I'll track one down."

"Let me call my aunt and see if she has one," he said.

"Oh, that would be great! Thank you!"

I hung up the phone and quickly ran back upstairs to put on a little makeup before he showed up. I didn't know what Gabriel and I were doing, but I liked him. I enjoyed spending time with him and didn't want to scare him off with my fresh-out-of-the-shower look. The man was too fast. He was there before I knew it. I took a last look in the mirror and declared it would have to be good enough. I flew back downstairs to greet him.

"Good morning!" I said, pulling open the door, greeting him with a big smile.

His warm grin sent a dash of joy through me. I couldn't explain it. It was just a happy, bubbly feeling. It was foreign, but lovely.

"Here are the tapes. I'm so sorry I forgot about them last night. Aunt Coral didn't have a VCR, sorry."

"It's okay. I'll find one. Thank you so much for bringing them by. I really appreciate it."

He looked at me, and I got the feeling he wanted to say something.

"Doing anything tonight?" he asked, sheepishly.

I smiled. "I don't think so. Are *you* doing anything?"

"Nope, not unless you agree to meet me for a sandwich at the deli."

I chuckled. "This place could really use a diner or somewhere other than the coffee shop in the post office that's also the deli."

He shrugged. "It adds to the charm of Lemon Bliss."

"I suppose."

"So, sandwiches for dinner, tonight?"

"Sounds fabulous."

"One of these days, I'll have you over to my house and I'll make dinner," he said with that disarming grin.

"Gabriel," I started.

He held up his hands. "I know, I know, you're not going to be around long. Got it, but in the meantime, we can have some fun, together. Right?"

"Right. I'm sorry, I know I keep saying that. I probably sound like a snob. I don't dislike Lemon Bliss, it's just I made a life away from here," I tried to explain.

"Don't worry about it. I understand. I really do."

The man was too good to be true. "Thank you."

"So, dinner?"

"Yes. Call me when you're done working. I'm sure I'll be here, doing nothing."

"Sounds good. I'll see you tonight," he said before jogging down the steps to his truck.

I took the box of tapes and set them on the coffee table. I had to find a VCR. The tapes were practically screaming at me to watch them. Unfortunately, they would have to wait for now. If only I were a witch. Then I could conjure up a VCR or at least that's what I assumed witches did. My extent of witchcraft knowledge was limited to what I'd seen on television, although these days that meant I had plenty of examples. If only they were more than fiction.

After a quick breakfast, I set out on a mission to find a VCR since no amount of wiggling my nose produced one. I checked with the guy at the deli to see if he knew of anyone in town who had one I could borrow. It was a dead end. It was off to Ruby Red to find a VCR. I was prepared to go all the way to New Orleans if I had to.

Thankfully, I didn't have to, but it took me stopping at three different stores only to finally find one at a thrift store. I drove home, so excited I had to fight my urge to speed. I was dying to see what was on those tapes. I hoped I could prove George wrong.

Once home, I tidied up, just in case Gabriel would be coming back home with me. I was a little nervous and anxious at the same time. Gabriel would be in grandma's house. Well, my house, but if my mom was right and her spirit was hanging out, I didn't need a witness.

I dusted off the small coffee table, stopping to stare down at the tapes. Would they confirm my suspicions or exonerate my mother and Lila?

# CHAPTER 10

$\mathcal{T}$he doorbell rang in the middle of my cleaning frenzy. I knew I was cleaning because I was stressed. It helped me think. I needed to think about what to do. What would I do if I discovered something incriminating on those tapes.

I blocked it out and went to the door, hoping it wasn't that awful man George.

"Mom," I said, opening the door. "What brings you here?"

"We need to talk. We didn't end things on a good note yesterday."

"You're right. You surprised me."

She walked into the living room, glanced at the box of video tapes, but didn't ask about them. I didn't know what I would have said if she had.

"I know you have a date tonight, so I won't keep you," she started.

"How do you know that? How does everyone always know where I am or what I'm going to be doing? It's downright weird," I muttered.

She didn't answer. Only smiled. She sat down on the couch and patted the seat next to her. "Sit."

I plopped down on the couch and waited.

"Have you had time to think about what I told you?" she asked.

I looked down at the rug under the table. "I've thought about it, but I don't know what I believe."

"I'm glad you're at least giving it some thought. I'm sure you have some questions. I want you to know you can talk to me. I'm here. Ask me anything."

I scoffed. "I don't know what questions to ask. I don't know if I'm totally on board with the idea of witchcraft."

"It isn't like that."

"What is it like?"

"Well, for starters, we are normal people. Each of us has gifts, some are the same, some are unique. Some of us can write spells while others are far more powerful than others. We avoid dark magic. That is far too dangerous. Doing things that bring us personal gain, like wealth, love or even happiness is frowned upon. Those spells always have a way of backfiring."

"Like Coral?"

"Yes, like Coral. We had been warned, but we were young and immature."

"Why wouldn't you tell me about any of this before?"

"Honestly, I wanted to so many times, but your grand-mother felt it best you didn't know. The coven agreed we would not tell the next generation until we were confident you were ready to handle it. We couldn't have a repeat of Coral's indiscretion. There is too much temptation when you're that young and dealing with typical teenage stuff," she explained.

I leaned back against the couch and stared up at the ceiling. "I believe you," I mumbled.

"I know."

I chuckled. "There were so many times I thought I was sick or crazy. I wish you'd have told me."

"I'm sorry, dear. I often wanted to tell you and teach you the ways, but I couldn't. I was terrified our secret would be exposed. It was too much of a risk."

"How come it was too much of a risk for my generation and not yours?" I asked.

She shook her head. "Because my generation was careless. We put everything in jeopardy. We had to go underground. It was the only way to protect our families."

"I get it. I think. Sometimes, I get what I guess are feelings. Like I can sense when something is going to happen. I can't know exactly what it is, but I don't know, it's hard to explain," I said, realizing I sounded crazy.

My mom was smiling and nodding. "The gift of premonition. I've always told you to listen to your instinct. That *is* your instinct."

"What about a tingling in my hands?"

"It's all part of your gift. I would love to teach you more about it and help you learn how to use those gifts. I know I'm a little late, but I want you to realize this is a gift and not a curse."

I wasn't so sure I was ready to start using the so-called gifts, but it was a relief to know there was an explanation for the weird feelings and happenings I had experienced occasionally. As much as my practical brain told me my mother's fantastical tale was a complete fabrication, I couldn't. Deep down I knew it was true. I had always suspected I was different than other people and now there was an explanation. A far-fetched one, but it was something to hold onto.

"I'll have to think about that, for now let's just accept it for what it is and worry about teaching me later. Mom, I need to ask you about the men who were in town. The supernatural investigators."

"What about them?"

"The man who died, did you know him?"

Her lack of an immediate denial worried me. "I didn't know him. I knew of him."

"Did you speak with him at all?"

"Not really, not more than I would talk to another visitor to town," she said, hedging in a way that made me even more nervous.

"But you talked with him and his partner George Cannon?"

She wouldn't look at me. Her eyes traveled around the room. I knew her too well. She was choosing her words carefully. "Yes, I talked to them both."

"About?"

A dainty shrug. "This and that. They spoke to many people in town."

"Why, Mom? Please, tell me why those men thought Lemon Bliss of all places would be somewhere worth visiting. Why did they spend money and resources to conduct an investigation if they didn't think there was something to find?"

"I can't speak for them."

I growled in frustration and jumped off the couch. "You know something. You dragged me into this! I deserve to know what's going on!"

"Dear, it's all being handled. There is nothing for you to worry about."

I spun around, staring at her with my mouth hanging open. "Oh, that totally settles it. I won't worry about it because you have it handled. I got called down here because the sheriff thinks I know something about a man dying in a factory that has my name on the deed. I could be facing all kinds of criminal charges for neglect or worse—murder!"

My mom waved a hand through the air, her charm

bracelets tinkling with the movement. "You don't have to worry about a thing."

I rolled my eyes. "You know that only makes me worry more. I received a phone call earlier, from the dead guy's partner. He made some threats. He also told me he has proof you and Lila have been visiting the factory pretty often. Is that true?"

"What kind of proof?"

"That wasn't the question, Mom!"

"People make threats all the time. People always assume they know something," she casually responded.

Nothing ever got her riled up. She was cool as a cucumber.

"Why is there such a fascination with that old factory?"

Her answer shocked me. "It's where the coven used to meet. For decades, the factory was the meeting place for our coven. We would practice our magic in the factory, away from the prying eyes of the public. My grandmother and mother designated the factory a safe place for witches to use their magic. It was our haven of sorts," she said with a wistful sigh.

I stared at her, stunned. It was true. She admitted to being in the factory, but was it recent, or had she been refer-ring to years past?

I cleared my throat. "Mom, have you been going there? You and Lila and the rest of the ladies? Is it still your meeting place?"

She waved another hand through the air, as if she could wipe away the question. "I don't know what you're talking about. I told you, it was established many, many years ago. There's a reason your grandmother built that factory there. Before that, the property was where the coven used to meet for centuries. Those were the good, old days. Our coven has been forced to hide. We can no longer meet so publicly."

"Why would the supernatural investigators be interested in where the coven *used* to meet?"

"I imagine they were looking for proof of magic. Magic leaves behind evidence, I guess you could call it. The regular person couldn't see it or feel it, but a witch in touch with her powers would be able to sense it. Those investigators believed their machines could pick up on the trace left behind as well," she explained.

I slowly nodded my head, understanding more about what had happened. "You didn't want them to discover the factory and the leftover magic, or whatever you want to call it."

"Of course not! That would expose us all! If they believed there was something there, more investigators would come. Other witches would learn about the factory and would stomp all over our little town. We can't risk that kind of exposure! Not all witches practice good magic. There are plenty out there who tap into the dark magic. It could be very dangerous for us and the people who live here. Don't you see the risk involved?" she stressed.

"I suppose I do, but how did that man die?" I asked point blank, almost afraid of the answer.

"I can't say."

"You can't say or you won't say?" I asked.

"I can't," she said, tersely.

That wasn't much of an answer and only left me more suspicious. I couldn't believe my mother would ever harm anyone, but she was very passionate about protecting her secret. My stomach was in knots. If not my mother, could one of the other witches have taken it upon themselves to protect the coven and the history of Lemon Bliss?

She stood in front of me. "Violet, everything will be okay. We have to stick together. The investigator will get bored and realize there is nothing to investigate. He'll go home, and we'll be left in peace. Right now, we stick together, answer the sheriff's questions and say nothing about witches and covens."

"Are you asking me to lie?"

"Has he asked you if you're a witch?"

"No."

"Then, you're not lying. There's lying and there's not telling the whole truth. Harold doesn't need to worry about the witches. We aren't doing anything that concerns him. Everything is fine," she assured me again.

I nodded my head, knowing nothing was fine. My phone chirped, alerting me to a text. I quickly read it.

"I have to go, Mom. I'm meeting Gabriel tonight."

She smiled, "Yes, yes. You go. Have fun and don't worry about all this other stuff. It will work itself out."

I bit back the urge to laugh. It would work itself out all right, but it could very well end up with someone sitting in a prison cell. It wasn't long before my mind leapt back to the fact the main suspects were witches. Would they use a spell to get out of prison? Could they charm their way out of a murder rap by casting a spell on their accusers?

My head was spinning with the many possibilities. I really needed to brush up on witchcraft, and figure out what was real and what was make believe.

"I'll talk to you tomorrow. I'll want to hear all about your date!" She smiled as she headed for the door.

I stared at her, my brow furrowed in disbelief. How could she be so calm and casual? The more I learned, the more I believed my mother was involved with the death. That wasn't a good feeling to have. Why wouldn't my gift work now? If only it could give me a premonition telling me everything was okay and I wasn't surrounded by a town full of murderers.

Clearly, it didn't work on demand. Or at least I didn't know how to use it on demand. If this all went away and life went back to normal, I would ask my mom if there was a way to use the premonition thing when I needed it.

I laughed aloud into the room. I had gone from being a non-believer to a practicing witch in the span of twenty-four hours. Lemon Bliss was making me a crazy woman. I could've used some of my grandmother's lemon tea to take the edge off.

# CHAPTER 11

*I* walked into the Crooked Coffee and looked for Gabriel. He was seated at our table. I had dubbed it our table since it is where we'd had coffee together the last time. I much preferred sharing a table with him than thinking about witches and murder.

"Hi," I said, slipping into the chair across from him.

"I was worried you might stand me up."

"No. Definitely not. My mom stopped by."

He arched a brow. "How did it go?"

I let out a long sigh. "Better than before, I guess. Things are still a little tense, but we'll work through it."

"Good. Do you know what you want?"

"I think I'll have a soup and salad. What about you?"

He laughed. "I'm starving. I am going to get one of their giant sandwiches."

"Don't let me stop you."

We stood and walked to the counter to place our order. The sandwiches were made fresh, but the salads were the prepackaged kind and the soup I suspected came from one of those big industrial size cans. I didn't mind. As we ordered, I realized just how hungry I was.

We chatted about his job while we waited, and once again, I was surprised at how easy it was to talk to him. It was as if I had known him for years rather than just a couple of days. When our number was called, I jumped up to grab our tray.

"What'd your Mom have to say?" he asked, after he had eaten about a quarter of his sandwich.

"Not a lot." I took a deep breath, a little unsure if I should tell him everything my mom had said, but I figured he knew about the witches, so that would be safe. "She did tell me the factory was an old gathering spot for witches."

"Really? I guess that explains why the supernatural guys were in there."

"Oh, I didn't tell you, George Cannon called me today."

"Who's that?"

"He's one of the supernatural investigators. He was making some pretty serious accusations and I think he was trying to intimidate me."

Gabriel stopped, his sandwich halfway to his mouth. "What?"

"Not like that. At least I don't think so. He's pretty upset over his friend's death. He's convinced my mom is involved somehow. I think he actually insinuated she committed murder," I whispered.

His eyes went big. "Wow."

I chuckled, wiping my mouth. "I don't know. I think she may be involved in some way. I can't imagine her hurting anyone, but I think she and her friends know more than they're letting on. Maybe it was an accident?"

Gabriel shrugged. "I don't know. Your mom doesn't seem the type."

I didn't want to tell him everything, including the part about me and my mother being witches. Not just yet. It was more than enough for me to get used to the crazy idea. For now, it was good enough that he knew about his aunt.

"What if they had something to do with it?" I asked in a low voice.

Gabriel didn't get a chance to answer. Harold grabbed a chair and pulled it up to our little table. "I'm glad I ran into you," he said.

I stared at him in disbelief. Did the people in this town have no manners? No idea of personal space or when it was appropriate to sit down at another person's table?

"What's up, Sheriff?"

"Call me Harold. Everyone calls me Harold. Only strangers call me Sheriff, and since you are a local and living here, you can call me Harold as well."

"I'm not living here," I reminded him.

Gabriel grinned. "She's only staying here a couple of days, Harold."

It was sarcasm. Obviously, everyone had grown tired of my declarations and now it was a bit of a joke.

"Why were you looking for me?" I asked.

He leaned back in his chair. "I wanted to update you on the investigation. I know you're chomping at the bit to get out of here," he winked at Gabriel.

I rolled my eyes. "And?"

"Well, I'm about ready to wrap it up. I need to interview a couple more people, but I don't think you'll need to be here more than another day or two. I'm leaning towards foul play, but the list of suspects is pretty long. I've ruled you out, but unfortunately, your Mom is still at the top of the list."

I let out a long sigh and rubbed my brow where I could feel a tension headache coming on. "Why though? What makes you believe she is a suspect?"

"She has access to the building, and I know your mother pretty well. I know she's hiding something from me."

"That doesn't make her a murderer," I pointed out.

"No, it doesn't, but it might make her an accomplice." Harold shrugged a shoulder and stared at me intently. "Has she said anything to you? Mentioned why she would be visiting the factory?"

I looked at Gabriel, silently asking if I should reveal what I knew. He gave a very slight shake of his head.

"No."

"You don't sound like you're too sure about that."

"I don't know anything that could help you. I know my mother and I don't believe she would ever be involved in any type of crime. I think you know that as well," I said in a haughty tone.

That seemed to hit home. "I thought I knew her," he mumbled.

"Sorry, Harold, I don't think Violet or I can help you, tonight," Gabriel spoke up.

Harold looked at him before nodding his head. "Fine, I'll let you two enjoy your dinner. Violet, I know it's an imposition, but if you could stick around a couple more days that'd be great. Your Mom may need your support," he added.

"It's almost the weekend, the busiest time of the week at my shop," I pointed out.

"Sorry about that, but I'm sure you've got someone to handle things for you, right?"

The way it was said made it quite clear that he didn't care whether I did or didn't. He wanted me here and that was that.

"Yeah, I guess I do. But, if you can't give me anything by Saturday, Harold, I will leave. If you think there is something I need to answer for, or my mother needs to answer for, you'll have to speak to my lawyer."

Harold grinned. It wasn't exactly the response I had been looking for with my veiled threat. "Honey, if I had a dollar for every time someone threatened me with the lawyer line

I wouldn't need to wear this ugly uniform every day. You get yourself a lawyer. Make sure your mom has a good one, too, because if this turns out to be what I think it will, she is going to need a very good one to keep her out of prison."

He spun on his heel and walked out of the deli. I stared after him. I knew there was a possibility she would be on the hook for the crime, but hearing him actually say it was disturbing.

I turned to Gabriel. "Do you think she'll get charged with murder?"

"I hope not. We need to find out what happened that night."

"The tapes. I still have those tapes. I didn't have time to watch them today."

"Did you find a VCR?"

I laughed and told him of the wild goose chase I had gone on in my hunt for the antique. We returned to our food, eating in silence.

"Wouldn't it be better if my mom just came clean about the factory being an old witch gathering place? If she won't, maybe I should."

He choked on the drink of soda he had just taken. "No. Definitely not a good idea."

"Why not? It would explain why the investigators were interested in the place," I reasoned.

"Harold would have to include that information in his report. Can you imagine what would happen if that became public knowledge?"

I grimaced as a picture of the future of Lemon Bliss flashed into my head. With the recent interest in the super-natural, including all things vampire and witch related, it would definitely create a bit of hysteria. My mother kept a low profile, but with enough digging, it wouldn't be long before people figured out she was the descendant of the factory owner.

My name was on the deed and I would certainly be dragged into the mess. While there would probably be a huge group of people who envied and admired those who were real witches, or could claim witches in their family history, there was also the other side of the coin. A much more dangerous side.

"I guess you're right. What do you know about the factory?" I asked, wondering if he had more of the history than I did. Clearly, I had been sheltered my entire life, while Gabriel had been told all about the witches.

"I know witches haven't had it easy in general. History proves that. My mother told me stories about a coven that lived in this area in the early nineteen-hundreds. After the Salem witch trials, witches were much more careful, but according to my mother, there were some who were far too bold."

"What about that coven?" I asked, intrigued because I knew that would have been the coven my great-great-grandmother and so on down the line would have been a part of.

"Apparently, they found themselves embroiled in a murder investigation as well. It was rumored the witches had killed a man who was threatening to expose them. Back then, people weren't as accepting. They faced criminal charges as well as being run out of town."

"Another murder?" I asked in surprise. My mother had glossed over that little tidbit of information.

He nodded his head. "I don't remember the circumstances, but I know several of the witches were under suspicion. It changed the way they practiced their magic. As I understand it, that's when the factory became their secret clubhouse," he joked.

"Makes sense, I guess," I mumbled.

I needed to ask my mom about that incident. It would explain why she was so desperate to hide the truth now.

"You want dessert?" he asked.

"What are our options?"

He chuckled. "I saw a nice, big brownie. We can split it."

"Sounds good to me."

While he went up to procure our chocolate feast, I pondered over the new information. It was a lot like putting together a puzzle. I had some of the pieces, but not all. I needed to watch those tapes. I had a feeling they would tell me more than anyone in this town would. If I found real evidence incriminating my mother, I would have to decide what to do. No matter what my suspicions were, I couldn't believe she would actually kill a man, but what if the death were the result of a spell? It could have been Lila that cast the spell and my mom was covering for her to protect the coven.

I groaned thinking about the many possibilities, all of them leading back to my mother and her friends.

"That bad, huh?" Gabriel said, taking his seat at our table.

"I was just thinking about the situation. I wish I could go back in time and forget any of this ever happened. I would be at my bakery and living my regularly scheduled life."

"Not me."

"Not you, what?"

"I'm kind of glad this all happened."

"I don't think that man's family would agree."

"I don't wish death on anyone, but I'm glad you were forced to come here. I may have never met you if he hadn't met an untimely death."

I looked at him, and as much as I wanted to say he was wrong, I agreed with him.

"Don't tell anyone," I said, leaning forward and lowering my voice, "but, I think I'm glad I got dragged down here, too."

He grinned and took a bite of the brownie.

# CHAPTER 12

*I* needed to get to bed. I was exhausted, yet far too anxious to sleep. I had to see what was on those tapes. I was terrified I would see something horrible, but also hoping against the odds I would find something that proved my mother innocent on all counts. I didn't want to see her wearing prison orange. The woman could pull off some eccentric looks, but an orange jumpsuit was not going to work for her.

I changed into my shorts and t-shirt and settled in on the couch to watch some videos. I realized after about fifteen minutes of watching the first tape that the camera was set to turn on when it detected motion. The time stamp on the bottom corner of the screen attested to that fact.

Though I saw nothing each time, I assumed it was likely dust being stirred up that caused enough motion for the camera to turn on. The first tape was a complete let down and I started to think I was wasting my time. This was probably why the tapes had been left behind. There was nothing to see.

I popped in the next tape and rubbed my eyes, trying to

wipe away the sleep. I could feel something was here, I just wasn't sure what. The only way to find it was the old-fashioned way. I had to see it to believe it.

I blinked, rubbed my eyes and rewound the tape. I stood inches from the television, wanting to make sure I saw what I thought I saw.

"Oh no," I murmured into the empty room. "Oh no. Oh Mom."

I watched my mother walk into the factory and head towards the back on the bottom floor. There had to be a dozen cameras around the factory, which was a little disturbing. How could my mother not realize she had been caught?

I stood in front of the TV and gasped when I saw Lila walk in and head out of the camera's view in the same direction as my mother. The cameras bounced around from one area to the next, but there was no sign of them. It was as if they disappeared. A short few minutes later, Magnolia and Coral could be seen walking in together. They appeared to be laughing and chatting as if it was completely normal for them to be inside an abandoned factory in the middle of the night.

I checked the time stamp. It was just after midnight a week before the man had been killed. George Cannon hadn't been lying. My mother and her friends had been caught. I had the proof right in front of me.

Several more tapes revealed the same thing. My mother and her friends sneaking in the back of the factory and spending anywhere from thirty minutes to several hours somewhere off camera. It explained the footprints we saw in the dirt that day, but it didn't explain what they were doing.

I shut off the TV and headed upstairs. I was exhausted. It was after one and I needed to get some sleep. The tapes only proved my mother had been at the factory. There was no smoking gun or proof she hurt the man. Of course, I hadn't watched all of the tapes, yet, and wasn't certain what I would find when I did. I closed my eyes and tried to block it all out.

I managed to drift off to sleep, dreaming about witches, brooms and cauldrons.

As usual, I woke early. My eyes felt like sandpaper had been run over them a few times. I tried to go back to sleep, but it was pointless. My brain was in overdrive, trying to solve the mystery of my mom's involvement with the supernatural investigator's death.

I stumbled into the shower, hoping it would revive me. Not much luck there, which meant I was going to require copious amounts of caffeine and sugar. I really could have gone for one of my cream-filled doughnuts. My bakery was famous for them.

I yanked open the kitchen cupboards, looking for sugar. If I was going to stay here another day, I had to get some real food in the place. I was cranky, tired and bleary-eyed by the time I pulled up in front of Crooked Coffee. I probably should have had a warning label on my forehead.

"Hi," I mumbled to the young man behind the counter. "Coffee and an éclair."

"We don't have éclairs."

I pulled my sunglasses down and glared at him with my beet-red eyes. "Fine. Give me a doughnut with frosting. I don't care what kind."

"Someone's a little cranky this morning."

I groaned. I was not in the mood for this. I took a deep breath, promising myself I couldn't hit or snap at anyone, including Lila who came walking in the entrance moments after I did. "Good morning, Lila."

"Dear me, you look a little rough."

"Thank you. That's the look I was going for," I replied.

She took a step back. "Oh my."

I turned around and grabbed my coffee and doughnut from the cashier and made to leave, but Lila stopped me.

"Is everything okay, dear?"

"No. Excuse me, please. I need to get going."

"Where are you off to in such a hurry this morning?"

I still had my sunglasses on, so I hoped she couldn't see my eye roll. "I have a few things to take care of."

She stepped out of the way as I pushed past her and out the door. I had no idea where I was going. I'd intended to drink my coffee in the shop, but should have known that peace and quiet was not to be had there. Someone was *always* there and I was beginning to think I had some sort of homing beacon implanted on me.

I sat in my car for a few minutes, sipping my coffee. I watched as Lila made her way out, then quickly started my car and backed out of the spot. I had told her I was in a hurry, so I'd better act like it.

I drove down Crooked Street, debating where to go. I didn't want to go back to the house right away. Not yet.

An idea occurred to me and I took the first right and headed out of town. I parked in front of the old blue house and smiled. I loved this place.

I got out of the car, already feeling better. When Magnolia pushed open the screen door and stepped outside, I smiled and waved.

"Violet Broussard! I'm so glad you came by! I was hoping I'd see you while you were in town," she said with a warm smile, walking towards me.

"I'm sorry I didn't come by sooner."

"Come inside. You have to tell me everything. Your mom says you own a bakery?"

I nodded. "Yes, I do. It's doing pretty well."

We walked inside where she invited me to have a seat. "Do you want me to freshen up that coffee?"

"Please, I'm beat."

"You look like it. What's wrong? Is your grandmother's spirit keeping you up at night?"

I almost dropped the empty cup in my hand. "What?"

Magnolia gave me that smile I remembered from when I was younger. She used to babysit me quite a bit. Her daughter, Daphne, and I had been friends and spent a lot of time together. Whenever we were up to something, Magnolia always knew and always gave us that same smile.

"Your mom said she spoke with you about the family secret."

I took a deep breath and exhaled slowly. "Yes, she did, which is why I'm here."

"Let me get that coffee and we can talk," she said, taking my cup and heading into the kitchen.

I looked around her house. It was small, cozy and inviting. She wasn't a rich woman. Like all the other women my mother was friends with, she had been a single parent. My mother's friends had a hard time holding onto husbands. I hoped I didn't inherit that particular trait.

She sat down and patted my knee. "Here you go, sweetie. What's worrying you?"

I didn't want to come right out and tell her, but I needed to see how much she was willing to share with me. I had already seen the evidence on the tapes. Magnolia visited the factory and was just as suspicious as the rest.

"I don't know if anything is worrying me, but I am worried about this supernatural investigator. Do I need to worry?"

"I think your mom is handling things. There's really nothing any of us can do until Harold decides if it was a murder or an accident," she said, with resignation.

"What if he decides it is murder?"

"Nothing we can do but be prepared."

"Why would you need to be prepared?"

She looked down at her hands. "You just never know. There are some rumors and well, you know the rest."

She was hedging. None of these women were going to be straight with me. It was infuriating.

"Magnolia, tell me something. How far would you go to protect your secret and the secrets of your friends?"

She appeared lost in thought for a moment. "I don't really know. I know I would do everything in my power to keep our families safe. Sometimes, you have to do things you would rather not for the greater good. What good would it do anyone for our secret to be exposed and flaunted all over some cable television show?"

It was not the answer I was expecting. "I don't know. I don't think I would murder anyone over it."

Magnolia chuckled. "Well, I don't think any of us would, but you never know until you walk a mile in another person's shoes."

The door swung open and Daphne came in. "Violet?"

I stood and walked towards her to embrace her. "Daphne! It has been too long! How are you?" I asked, genuinely happy to see her.

"I'm great! What are you doing here?"

"I'm in town for a couple days and I thought I'd stop by and visit your mom. Are you living back here?"

She nodded. "Yep, came home a couple months ago, only to find everyone had disappeared."

"I'm sorry, I didn't know you were living here. I would have tracked you down earlier. We have to catch up!"

"Are you doing anything now?" she asked.

I shrugged. "Not really. I'm hurrying up and waiting."

She nodded her head while furrowing her brow. "Oh, the investigation. I'm sorry you had to come back for this. It's really sad someone died in the old factory, but I don't know why Harold is making such a big fuss about it. As if your mom would ever hurt anyone."

I kept my opinion to myself and didn't say any more. Clearly Daphne wasn't privy to all the information. "Want to grab some coffee?" I asked.

She looked at the cup in my hand. "Looks like you've already been drinking coffee."

I laughed. "Trust me, I need more, plus it's before noon. Coffee before noon and espresso after noon. That's my rule."

"I'm in. Crooked Coffee?" she asked.

Though they had the best coffee in town, I hadn't had good luck with the coffee shop. Every time I set foot in the place, I was disturbed by some busy body.

"Is that really the only coffee shop in town?" I asked.

"No, but it's the only place most people get coffee. There's the diner, but I don't think they're open this early."

I sighed and gave in. "All right, Crooked Coffee it is. I'll meet you over there?"

"Yep, I'll be over there about five minutes behind you. Save me a seat," she winked.

I laughed. The place wasn't usually too crowded. That is until I showed up.

# CHAPTER 13

$\mathcal{T}$he table I had become so fond of was taken, forcing me to take one by a window instead. It wasn't as though it mattered if anyone could see me through the window anyway. Anyone who wanted to find me always seemed to know where I was regardless. I ordered another stout cup of coffee and hoped it would finally satisfy my craving for caffeine. After liberally adding sugar, I sipped my coffee and stared out the window, lost in thought.

"I'm here!" Daphne said, slightly out of breath as she sat down. "Mom got to chatting and before I knew it, ten minutes had passed. I'll be right back," she said, getting up and going to the counter.

I watched her move and wished I had a fraction of her energy. Daphne's almost black hair was pulled back in a slapdash ponytail. She shared her mother's bright blue eyes and willowy build.

Returning to the table, she sat down with a flourish. "Tell me everything."

I burst out laughing. "That could take a while."

"Okay, let's start with the basics. Boyfriend? Married?"

"Neither. You?"

"Long story and I don't really want to talk about it when I'm in a good mood. How's your bakery?"

"Good, really good, which reminds me I need to call my assistant manager today and check in. What are you doing these days?"

She rolled her eyes. "I'm a mess. Right now, I'm working at the bank in Ruby Red. I worked as a home caregiver in New Orleans. Before that I waitressed and before that I worked as a photographer's assistant. Nothing ever fits. I feel like I'm lost and can't find my way."

"I'm sorry. Have you tried one of those tests that tells you what kind of career you should go into?"

She laughed, "Just the one we did in school."

I shrugged a shoulder and offered a sympathetic look. "I'm sorry. You're still young. You'll find something you love."

She turned the coffee cup in her hand. "Violet, I know."

I drank my coffee. "Good. What do you think you'll do?"

She shook her head. "No. I mean, I *know*," she repeated, stressing the word.

I stopped the cup midway to my mouth. "You know?"

Daphne glanced around the semi-empty coffee shop. "My mom told me that your mom told you."

I felt like we were speaking in code, and I didn't like it. I didn't have the patience to try and keep it up. Not today. Not on a day I was barely able to keep my eyes open as it was.

"What are you talking about Daphne?"

"The witch thing. The fact that we're witches," she whispered.

"Oh." At a loss, all I could manage with that single syllable.

"I was shocked, too. I mean, witches! I thought that stuff

was only in books. I didn't believe her at first, but it didn't take long for it all to make sense. Things that had happened when we were little all started to add up. I'm still kinda mad she didn't tell me sooner, but I understand why."

I found myself nodding my head. "Yes!" I enthusiastically agreed. "So many things could have been explained if we'd known the truth. I guess part of me is glad I didn't know, but the other part of me hates that I didn't know sooner."

"Pretty crazy, though, huh?"

"It is. So, are you going to tell me why you're back here? I have time."

Daphne rubbed her face with her hands. "Ugh, well, the fact is I had nowhere else to go."

My heart went out to her as tears filled her eyes. "I'm sorry," I said softly. "You don't have to tell me if you don't want to. I understand."

She wiped her eyes and shook her head before taking a sip of coffee. "No, it's fine. My husband is a cheating jerk. I came home from work early one day and caught him in bed with another woman."

"Oh no, I'm sorry."

She started laughing, but it was a bit of a maniacal sound. "It wasn't the first time. That's how pathetic I am. I caught him twice before. I don't even want to know how many others there were that I didn't catch him with."

"That's terrible. I'm sorry, but it sounds like you're better off without him."

"I agree. Mom is letting me crash with her until I can get on my feet, again. I feel like such a child having to run home to mommy."

"That's what moms are for."

"Enough about me," she waved a hand through the air. "Rumor has it you and Gabriel have been hooking up."

My eyes practically popped out of my head. "What? No! Hooking up? Who said that?"

She was giggling, "You know how much our mothers gossip."

"Lila more like it," I grumbled.

"She has definitely been fueling the fire, but it's all of them. I think they sit around talking about us all the time."

"Probably. I guess it's better than casting spells and giving poor unsuspecting women acne," I joked.

"Oh my gosh, she told you about that! Isn't that funny. Coral ruined it for us. Just think what we could have done to Gretchen!" she grinned.

"Ugh, I would have put a giant wart on her nose if I could have. She would have deserved it."

"Okay, let's get back to Gabriel. I've seen him around a few times. He's hot. What's the deal there?"

I shrugged, not sure how to answer the question. I was starting to really like him, but he lived here and I lived two hours away. I couldn't imagine how difficult it would be to try a long-distance relationship.

"I don't know. We've been out a couple of times, and we seem to click. It's weird. I've never really experienced that with anyone before," I admitted.

She was smiling and nodding, "You like him."

"I do."

"Good, then stay."

"What?"

"Stay here. God knows, this town could use a bakery. You could open a bakery here and stay. You could have your cake and eat it too," she grinned. "Get it. Have your cake and eat it too, Gabriel is the *too*."

I had to laugh at that. "Cute, but I can't just pull up stakes and start a whole new bakery. It takes money, equipment, I'd need a building and so on. It took me years to get my bakery established and running at a profit."

"I'll help. I have a feeling Gabriel would too. Your mom,

my mom and the others. We're your family. Come home, Violet," she said softly.

I shook my head, but inside, she had planted a seed. I already had a place to live, mortgage free, which would mean I wouldn't be too financially dependent on the bakery turning a profit the first few months.

"I don't know, Daphne. It's a lot to think about. Gabriel and I have spent very little time together, really. I'm not ready to move here to be with a man I don't even know that well. There may not even be a future for us."

"You won't know unless you try."

"What if, you know," I said, bobbing my head.

"I know what?"

"The witch thing. What if he finds out and wants nothing to do with me?"

That seemed to take the wind out of her sails. She leaned back in her chair. "Oh."

"Exactly."

"His mom was a witch. It isn't like he isn't familiar with the whole thing. I don't think he'd run scared. Give him a chance."

"We'll cross that bridge when we come to it. For now, my focus is on this investigation," I said, steering the conversation back to a much safer topic.

She whistled low. "What a mess."

"Daphne, can I tell you something?"

"Sure, you used to tell me everything."

"You can't tell your mom," I said, looking her straight in the eye.

"I won't, but you are kind of freaking me out. What's going on?"

I took a deep breath and hoped I wasn't making a mistake. "Did you know your mom and the others have been going to the old lemon tea factory in the middle of the night?"

"What? Why would they do that?"

"I don't know. My mom, Lila and Coral were also making midnight visits. I found some tapes in the factory. I stayed up last night watching the surveillance tapes and saw it with my own two eyes."

"Where did you get surveillance tapes?" she asked, confusion all over her face.

"The supernatural investigators set up cameras all over the place. For whatever reason they left a box of tapes behind. Gabriel and I found them and I took them home."

"Why didn't you turn them over to the sheriff?"

I looked at her.

"Oh," she said with realization.

"Exactly. My mom is already under suspicion. What if she or one of the others did it?" I hissed.

"No way. None of them could hurt anyone. You know that."

"I thought I did, but I also didn't know I was a witch or that any of them were. My mom has told me repeatedly she would do whatever it took to protect the coven. What if she killed that man to keep him from exposing her?"

Daphne was shaking her head. "No way. I don't believe that for a second. There is no way she would ever do that. Why would she? I mean, if all of them are witches, couldn't they cast a spell or something and make the guy forget what he saw?"

That was a good point and one I hadn't thought of. "Good point."

"Did you see anything else on the tapes? I mean is there anything truly incriminating? Watching them come and go doesn't mean they actually murdered him."

"No, I didn't. I still have several more to go through. I'm almost afraid of what I'll see. What if I find out she did or Lila did something? I don't know if I could turn them in. I can't do that."

"Don't worry about what hasn't happened. Watch the rest of the tapes before you assume anything. Have you asked your mom about it?"

I rubbed my face, the caffeine burst was already wearing off. "No. I was up late last night and haven't had a chance to talk to her today."

"I can't tell you what to do, but if I were you, I'd finish watching those tapes before you confront her. Maybe instead of proving her guilt, you'll prove her innocence. Look for the positive instead of focusing on the negative," Daphne said with a bright smile.

Insert eye roll. "Since when did you become a Pollyanna?"

"Since I realized life is only as bad as you let it be. I've seen a lot of bad in my life and I don't want to anymore. Unless it is straight-up, horrible, I'm not going to see the bad anymore," she said as if believing it would make it so.

"It's worth a shot. I'll go home and watch the tapes and hope for the best. I just hope Harold stops focusing so much on my mom."

She checked her watch. "I have to get to work. I'll catch up with you this weekend. You'll still be around I hope?"

"I don't know for sure. I'm going to talk to Harold, I mean Sheriff Smith, and see where he's at. I don't feel like I'm actually doing anything. It seems silly for me to hang out indefinitely."

She stood and looked down at me. "I think you're doing something, you just don't know it yet."

I watched as she walked out of the shop before getting up and making my way back to my car. Daphne was right. I needed to quit being so negative. My trip to Lemon Bliss wasn't all that bad. I had met Gabriel. I learned I was a witch. Which I couldn't quite believe.

It wasn't all bad. Now, I just had to prove my mother was innocent of murder. How hard could that be?

# CHAPTER 14

$\mathcal{I}$ was dreading the phone call I had to make. Tara had probably given up on me. I certainly felt like I had abandoned her.

Once I was home, oddly enough I referred to my grandmother's house as home now, I called her.

"Hi," I said sheepishly.

She was quiet at first. "Hey, there. I'm going to forget what you look like."

"I know. I suck. I'm a horrible boss and friend. I've completely left you in the lurch."

"It's really okay. I did hire another employee though. I couldn't keep doing the long days by myself," she said, but I didn't hear irritation in her voice.

"Good. I'm glad. We've been talking about doing that forever. I'm so sorry. This is all such a mess."

"I understand. You can't exactly control how fast the police work."

I scoffed. "I wish. Slow isn't even the word for it. It isn't like this place is rife with crime, but this is a suspicious death, so it's kinda news around here. The sheriff seems intent on taking his time. I'm worried about leaving until he resolves this," I explained.

"Should I be worried?" she asked.

"No! Definitely not. I'll figure something out. I'll drive up on Monday, even if I have to come back that night, but I will be there."

"Sounds good. So, what else have you been up to in Lemon Bliss, Louisiana? I just love saying that name."

I giggled, happy to hear she wasn't upset with me. "Not a lot. I snuck into the factory and stole some surveillance tapes. I watched a bunch until way late last night, and I'm getting ready to watch the rest right now."

"You did what!" she shrieked. "Violet!"

"It's not as bad as it sounds. This place is very different. I don't think I'll get in the same kind of trouble I would if it was a real cop and a real investigation," I joked.

"Violet, the law is the law. Your sheriff may not be a big time cop, but I have a feeling he'd be upset if he knew you took evidence. You're walking a dangerous line. That is so unlike you," she added.

It was unlike me, but I couldn't exactly explain to her why it was so important I see the tapes. "I know. I guess I should probably turn them over."

"Yes, you should. Is that guy putting you up to this?"

"Gabriel? No. I mean he was with me and he knows about the tapes, but I put him up to it, and he just kind of went along with it."

"Violet, please be careful. I know you say it's a small town, but you are messing with serious stuff. Someone died in that factory. If you're going to be headed off to prison, I need to know."

"I'm not. It will all be fine. Look, I need to go, but I'll check in tomorrow and I *will* see you Monday, if not sooner," I promised, knowing I had no business making promises I couldn't keep.

"Take care and stay out of trouble!"

I laughed and hung up. She was right. Kind of. I would hand over the tapes, but I wanted to see for myself what was going on in the factory first. I was holding out hope that the investigators may have put up a new camera as the weeks went by. I was just as interested to see what my mother had been up to as the investigators were.

After watching several more tapes and seeing nothing exciting or interesting, I started to feel guilty. I shouldn't be watching the tapes. They were likely evidence in a murder case. I had no business playing amateur detective. Not to mention, they were boring as hell. There was nothing to see. Nothing, but static and dust. My eyes hurt from the strain of trying to see through the blackness. There was nothing there. Maybe the investigators thought they were capturing ghosts on film, but I saw nothing of the sort.

I turned off the tape, looked in the box to see three more that were unwatched and shook my head. I couldn't do it. The guilt felt like a boulder on my shoulders and I couldn't fathom the idea of watching another minute of tape. I had seen my mother and her friends coming and going several more times, but it was always brief blips before they disappeared. Maybe that's what the investigators were excited about. Could they have thought my mother and the other women literally disappeared?

I grabbed my phone and called the sheriff's office.

"Is Sheriff Smith in?" I asked when his secretary answered.

"Yes. Who's calling?"

"This is Violet Broussard. I really need to speak to him."

She put me on hold and I suddenly felt very nervous. He was likely going to be very angry. I'd discovered and withheld evidence. I had my defense prepared and readied myself for a long lecture and maybe even a night in jail. I really hoped it didn't come to that, but I had done something pretty bad.

"Miss Broussard, what can I do for you?" his deep voice came on the line.

I cleared my throat and took a deep breath. "I have some video tapes I think you may be interested in."

"What kind of video tapes?"

"Uh, they are videos from surveillance cameras that are or were set up in the factory."

"I thought you didn't have security out there?" he asked, suspicion in his voice.

"I don't."

"I see. So, where did you get these tapes?"

I hesitated. I was giving him the tapes, so I didn't need to give away my part in procuring the tapes. "I found them. Do you want them?"

"If they are related to my investigation, of course I want them. Can you bring them down now?"

I checked the time. "Yes, I'll be right down to drop them off," I stated, making sure he knew I wasn't going to sit through an interrogation. He was getting the tapes. That would have to be enough.

I took the box out to the car and made my way to the sheriff's department.

He was waiting for me and looked none too pleased. "Huh, look at that. A whole box of video tapes."

"Yes."

"What's on them?"

I considered denying I watched them, but had a feeling that would be futile. "Nothing that I saw."

"What did you see?"

"Nothing exciting. A lot of dust. A few shadows here and there," I lied.

"I assume these are from cameras that those investigators set up?"

"Yes. They look to be motion activated," I explained.

"And you just stumbled upon them?"

I looked down at my feet. "Basically."

"Were they in your grandmother's house?" he asked.

That was an option, but if I said that, I would be incriminating my mother. "No."

"I see."

I took a deep breath and met his eyes. "I'm going to go now."

I half-expected him to stop me. Slap handcuffs on me and toss me in some dark, dank cell where I would only be served bread and water before I was found out to be a witch and burned to death. Yes, I had an active imagination. I needed to sleep. My brain was mush.

"All right, thank you for doing the right thing, even if you did the wrong thing. I'll take a look. You know the drill; stick around in case I have any more questions."

I groaned. "Sheriff Smith, is that really necessary?"

"Yes, and unless you would like me to remind you that breaking into an active crime scene is illegal and stealing evidence is also illegal, I suggest you cool your jets and stick around town," he lectured.

"Of course, I understand," I replied, keeping my annoyance to myself.

Leaving the police station, I returned to my car. I knew I wasn't leaving Lemon Bliss, but it was still frustrating being told I needed to stick around. I needed to start thinking beyond the next day and get some food in the house.

Aiming my car to the small grocery store, I scanned the parking lot before getting out of the car. I wanted to get in and out, unnoticed if it all possible.

Instead of the little carry basket, I grabbed an actual cart. It was then I realized I was starving and craving a good, hot meal. The only problem was, I didn't cook. I baked, but cooking meals was not my thing. I could make cakes and pastries all day, but my cooking skills were basic. I'd never found it quite as fun as baking.

I pushed my cart to the freezer section and picked out a few frozen meals along with a few other quick meals. By the time I made it to the produce section, I realized my cart was close to full. Mother would tell me this is why a woman should never go grocery shopping when she was hungry or tired.

"My mom always told me the produce section was a great place to meet women," a husky, familiar voice cut through my perusal of the fruit section.

A smile curled my lips as I turned around to see Gabriel standing there, a basket in his hand. "Hi!"

"You looked like you were really serious about those melons," he teased.

"I was spacing out."

"You look exhausted. Did you stay up all night watching those tapes?"

I slowly nodded my head. "Yes, I did."

"Anything interesting?"

"Nope. Very boring," I said, not quite ready to tell him what I saw or where the tapes were now.

"I take it by that loaded cart you might be planning to stay a while," he said, looking at my cart full of snacks.

"I figured with as fast as the sheriff is moving with this investigation, I better be prepared for anything. What doesn't get eaten I can leave here for when I come to visit. I don't like being in a house with nothing to eat."

He chuckled. "Who does? I'm glad to hear you're planning on visiting."

I smiled. "I am, if I ever leave. Well, strike that. I'm leaving on Monday, no matter what the sheriff says. I need to get back and check on things at the bakery. If I need to come back again, I will."

Gabriel's gaze coasted over my face, but I couldn't quite

read if he had a reaction to my announcement. It wasn't as if it as news. I'd never planned to stay in Lemon Bliss.

"Do you want to grab dinner tomorrow night? One last hurrah before you leave?"

"I'd like that. Tonight, I am going to pop in one of these dinners, eat and pass out. I am absolutely dead on my feet."

"I understand. I was just picking up a few things myself. Want to meet for coffee in the morning? That is assuming you're up before nine," he joked.

"Ha! I wish I could sleep past six. I'll meet you there. What time?" I asked.

"Want to shoot for seven? That gives us plenty of time."

"Yes, I'll be there," I said with a smile.

"Okay, see you tomorrow. Go home and get some rest. Quit watching those tapes," he ordered.

I smiled and nodded, not correcting his assumption about the tapes. "Bye, Gabriel."

He drifted away and I went back to choosing the right melon. I was really going to miss him when I went home.

# CHAPTER 15

*A*fter a good nights' sleep, I woke up with the sun, feeling refreshed and ready for the day. I knew it wasn't just the sleep that had me in a good mood. I was excited for my coffee date with Gabriel. This should've made me wonder just what I was thinking, but I didn't quite feel like it.

Sorting through my meager clothing items, I put together an outfit. Grandma's old washer didn't work, which I'd discovered last night. If I were going to be spending more time in Lemon Bliss, I would need to get a new one for the house. With my shirt halfway over my head, I stopped. What was I thinking?

I was thinking as if I'd be here. A lot. It was as if it was already decided. I knew that, but some part of me was lagging behind and not quite on board with what was happening.

"Get with the program," I said to myself while looking in the mirror.

I could lead a double life. The drive wasn't that bad, I

reasoned. I could spend a few days down here every couple of weeks. Right?

I'd have to think about it some more. I wasn't sure what Gabriel and I were doing, but I felt like the relationship could go somewhere, if I was willing to put in the effort. He could drive up and see me as well.

"Slow down, turbo," I scolded myself.

I was getting way ahead of myself and already planning a relationship I wasn't sure would even happen. There was the chance he was simply being nice and keeping me busy while I was in town. One step at a time.

When I pulled up in front of Crooked Coffee, I wasn't surprised to find it was fairly busy. Most of the people who lived in town had to commute to outlying towns and even New Orleans. That meant they had to be up early and on the road, which made Crooked Coffee the hot spot for early morning commuters.

Gabriel was at a table that was dragged into the adjoining post office. I assumed this was part of the morning rush. The post office wasn't open, so the coffee shop could use the floor space to handle the influx of business. It was a good idea. If I wanted to open a bakery, I wondered if I could find a place big enough.

There I went again, making plans for a future that was not certain.

"Hey," I said, walking towards him, doing my best not to bump too many shoulders as I made my way through the cramped space.

"Glad you found me. This place is crazy this morning."

"Is it always this busy?" I asked.

He shook his head. "Not like this. There's a rodeo a couple towns over. These people are passing through."

"Oh, I see. Is one of those for me?" I asked hopefully, gesturing to the two cups of coffee on the table.

"Yes, I figured I better get one for you so you wouldn't

have to wait in line. I got regular coffee. I think that's what you normally get, right?"

"Yes, thank you." Slipping into the chair across from him, I was grateful we were out of the way of most of the crowd in the coffee shop.

"Did you get some sleep last night or did you stay up watching exciting surveillance tapes?" he grinned.

"Actually, I slept very well, better than I have in a long time."

"That's a bummer you didn't see anything on the tapes. I was hoping the cameras actually caught a ghost."

I looked down at my coffee and turned the cup in my hands. "I did see a little something."

"What? What did you see?" he asked excitedly.

"My mom, your aunt, Magnolia and Lila."

His eyes widened and he slowly shook his head. "No way," he breathed out.

"Yes way. They were coming and going all hours of the night. It was strange. Unfortunately, the cameras weren't placed in every corner of that massive building. They walked right out of the cameras' view, and I have no idea where they went or what they did," I explained.

"Wow. That's strange. I'm sure there's a reason for it. Did you ask your mom about it?"

"No," I said a little embarrassed.

"You have to talk to your mom."

"I went out to visit Magnolia. I wanted to see if she would admit to being there or maybe give me a clue about what they were doing there, but she didn't. Those women are tight-lipped."

"Lila isn't. Ask her," he replied.

"It doesn't matter now. Sheriff Smith has the tapes. He can ask them."

Gabriel's coffee cup paused inches from his mouth. "What?"

"I said Harold has the tapes. If he thinks they're worth questioning the women further, he will."

Gabriel put his cup of coffee down and looked me in the eye. "How did Harold know about the tapes?"

"I told him."

He nodded his head, as if he were encouraging me to say more. I didn't.

"Why?"

I shrugged a shoulder. "Because they were evidence."

He closed his eyes, his shoulders rising and falling with a deep breath. "How did he get the tapes?"

"I gave them to him," I said slowly as if he were the one having a hard time comprehending my words.

"Why would you do that?" he hissed.

I leaned back in my own chair, putting some distance between us. I didn't like his attitude. "Because it was the right thing to do."

"For who?"

"Um, it's an active investigation. It felt weird to keep them from Harold," I finally replied.

"You could have just landed your mother, my aunt and the others in a load of trouble."

I cocked my head to the side and studied him closely. "Do you know something you're not telling me?"

"No, but I know all of them and none of them would ever hurt anyone!" he exclaimed.

I glanced around the coffee shop, hoping no one heard him. "Keep your voice down. I don't know why you're mad at me. I did what I should have done from the very beginning."

He was shaking his head. "I'm surprised. I thought you took the tapes to protect your mother, not get her in more trouble."

"Gabriel, I watched all but a couple of the tapes. I didn't see anything that incriminated any of them. Yes, they were there in the factory, but I didn't see them killing a man. Why were they there? I did ask my mom if she had been, but she wouldn't give me a straight answer."

I watched as he slowly drank his coffee. His jaw was clenched. He was angry. I had managed to destroy a relationship in record time. Usually it took me a week or two before I chased a man away. I was getting better at it.

"I should probably get going," he mumbled.

I fought back the disappointment that blackened my earlier mood. "Okay. Gabriel, for what it's worth, I'm sorry I let you down. It certainly wasn't my intention. I'm not trying to hurt my mom or any of them. I had to do what I felt was right and that was giving those tapes to the sheriff. I couldn't live with myself if I held back key evidence. That man's killer needs to be brought to justice, even if it is my mother or someone I care about."

He ignored me and stood to leave. "I understand," he said, in a low voice. "I understand, but I don't agree with your decision."

I sighed, before looking up at him to see the disappointment in his eyes. "I'm sorry," I whispered.

He stared at me for several long minutes before leaving me alone at the table. I fought back the urge to chase after him. It was a sign. I didn't belong in Lemon Bliss. I had tumbled into some silly fantasy about finding a man worth picking up my whole life and moving for. Gabriel wasn't that man.

I sipped my coffee, not quite ready to leave yet. I didn't have anywhere to go or anyone to see. I had never felt so completely lost.

"You look like you just lost your puppy," Daphne said, plopping down in the chair Gabriel had just vacated. "I saw Gabriel outside. Is everything okay?"

I shrugged. "Sure. I made certain Gabriel won't call or want to have coffee again."

"What happened?" she asked, concern in her voice.

I unburdened my soul, telling her about the tapes I had turned over and how it had upset Gabriel.

"He'll get over it. You did the right thing. I mean, I hope my mother doesn't get hauled off to jail, but if she did something wrong, she needs to be held accountable. I think he'll see that as well," she assured me.

I waved a hand. "Oh, well. It wasn't like it was going to last anyway."

She started laughing. "That's where you're wrong. Judging by how upset both of you are over this little disagreement, I would say it is most definitely going to last. This is a relationship with potential. Don't throw it away."

"I don't know if I have the final say in that," I whined.

"Oh, sure you do. He's going to go to work, blow off some steam and I bet he'll be groveling by lunch," she winked.

I laughed. "I doubt that, but it would be nice if we could make up before I left, at least."

"Speaking of that, stay. Please," she begged, her hands put together in front of her as she looked at me. "Stay. Live here. You can open a bakery and I'll help. I'm great with bookkeeping, or you can show me how to bake or whatever. I'm at your service. It'll be fun. Come on!"

"Daphne, I can't open a business because it will be fun. It costs money."

"You have money. I know your grandmother's inheritance passed to you. Use it to invest in your future."

I shook my head. "I can't. I promised myself I wouldn't use that money unless it was a dire emergency. Besides, that's the money I used to open my first bakery. I don't want to dip into it again. The money is supposed to be passed down to my children," I explained.

She rolled her eyes. "You Broussard women sure are frugal. No wonder you're all rich."

I laughed. "You don't save money by spending it, besides, I don't know if a bakery would be successful here. I don't want to open a business and have it fail right away. That would crush my soul."

"It won't. Look at this place. We are in desperate need of a real bakery. The Crooked Coffee can go back to being a deli and a coffee shop. Let's face it; their sandwiches are awesome, but the bakery stuff there is just basic."

I thought about it for a few seconds. "Okay, I'll go home and crunch some numbers and do research on the area. I just don't see how there's a market for a bakery around here or a place to put it," I said.

"You leave that to me. I've got to get to work. I'll call you tomorrow and let you know what I find. I expect your report to be finished as well," she said in a mock stern voice.

I saluted her, "Yes, ma'am."

"Call Gabriel," she called as she walked out the door.

Everyone in the shop turned to look at me. I could feel myself blushing as I grabbed my coffee and left. I didn't need the entire town knowing Gabriel and I had a minor disagreement. I took the long way home, driving down some of the side roads and checking out the town. The idea of opening a bakery was exciting. I loved the thrill of trying something new, but I wasn't sure I had the stomach for it. I would definitely have to think on it.

# CHAPTER 16

My brain hurt after all the research and number crunching. I finally came to the conclusion that if I really wanted to, I could make a bakery work. It would mean long hours and would be a big risk, but I was convinced it was feasible. The key would be shipping out daily orders to nearby towns. No matter how I figured it, Lemon Bliss alone did not have the population to support a bakery.

I put away my laptop and meandered into the kitchen in search of a snack. There was a nice selection, which made me smile, as I remembered running into Gabriel at the grocery store. It wasn't long before that smile turned into a frown, once I recalled how things had ended that morning with him. Not good at all.

When I heard the doorbell, I immediately felt butterflies in my stomach. Gabriel!

I ran for the door, swung it open, prepared to apologize, but instead of Gabriel, I found my mother standing there.

"Mom! I wasn't expecting you."

She gave me a bit of a dirty look. "If you knew how to

use your powers better, you would have known," she snapped.

"Uh, okay. What's wrong?"

She pushed past me and walked into the living room. My mother didn't often get irritated, but I could tell when she was. At that moment, I could practically see waves of anger radiating off her.

Closing the door, I walked towards her, waiting for her to tell me what happened. When she turned around to face me, I saw anger mingled with hurt in her eyes. She didn't have to tell me. I already knew. Gabriel had told her what I'd done.

"Violet, I'm not mad at you for doing what was right, but how could you not talk to me first?"

"I don't know how much he told you, but I'd like to explain," I said, taking a seat in one of the antique wingback chairs.

She sat on the sofa. "He didn't tell me anything. Coral did."

"Oh," I muttered, realizing Gabriel had run straight to his aunt. I hadn't expected that, but I guess the family bond was far stronger than any little thing we had.

"You could've come to me," she said in a low voice.

"Mom, I tried. I asked you if you had been visiting the factory. When I saw not just you, but all of you on those tapes, I didn't know what to think," I tried to explain.

She gently shook her head. "You could have asked. I would have told you."

"Would you? Because every time I've asked a few questions about it, you get all vague," I said, jumping up, needing to pace.

"Yes, but that doesn't matter now. Coral has called an emergency meeting of the coven, tonight. We want you and Daphne there."

I spun around, my mouth hanging open. "What?"

"We think it's time you joined the coven and began to learn about who we are and what we're about. We've held too many secrets for too long. You don't trust us, and now that distrust may have cost more than we are willing to pay," she said, in a strained voice.

"Mom, I wasn't trying to hurt you or your, your coven!" I blurted out. "It was the right thing to do. You raised me to be an honest, law-abiding person and that's what I am. I couldn't take the guilt. I had to turn the tapes over."

"I understand. Please, we need you to be at the factory at midnight. Turn off your headlights and drive around the back. The door will be unlocked," she instructed.

I was immediately hesitant to go to the factory with them in the middle of the night. I had watched too many movies. Would they sacrifice me for exposing them?

"Oh stop!" she chided as she eyed me. "Quit acting like we're a bunch of monsters. No one is going to hurt you."

"How did you know what I was thinking? Were you reading my mind?" I said, stepping away from her.

She rolled her eyes. "My word you have an active imagination. I've got to go. I'll see you tonight," she said, and walked out the door, not waiting for me to agree or decline her invitation.

It wasn't an invitation, I realized. It was a demand. I had a feeling if I didn't show up, they would come and get me. A million thoughts ran through my head. Was I in danger? Should I flee and run back home? Did I dare call the sheriff and let him know what was happening?

I sat back down as the fear washed over me. I needed to get control of myself. I was jumping to conclusions without really knowing anything. This was my mother I was talking about. She would never hurt me. I hoped.

The rest of the day passed way too fast. I was a nervous wreck. I cleaned every room in the house, dusting and polishing away my apprehensions. By the time it was close to midnight, I had worked myself up into a serious frenzy. I had come to the conclusion it would be my last night on earth. The witches had to protect themselves and that meant getting rid of loose ends. I knew I couldn't hide. I had to face them and be ready to accept whatever they decided my fate was to be.

I drove to the factory alone. When I pulled behind the building, I saw two other cars. Either they had carpooled or not everyone was there. I took several deep breaths before getting out of my car on shaking legs. I managed to walk to the door and pull it open.

I screamed when Daphne appeared in front of me. My startled scream caused her to scream. "What's wrong!" she shouted.

"You scared me!"

She started giggling uncontrollably. "You scared me!"

"What are you doing sitting here in the dark?" I hissed.

"Waiting for you. Everyone else is waiting over there," she motioned with her hand.

I peered through the darkness, but I couldn't see anything. My heart was racing so fast I thought I would pass out. Daphne was acting normal, but it could be a ruse to soothe me into complacency. She grabbed my hand and started to move towards the back of the factory. This was the same way my mother had taken when I saw her on the videos.

"Good evening, Violet," I heard Coral say.

My stomach twisted into knots. She sounded so calm, normal even.

"Is everyone here?" Lila asked.

"Yes, let's go," my mother directed.

I clenched Daphne's hand in my own, terrified about what was to come.

"What's wrong with you?" she whispered.

"Ha, as if you don't know," I shot back.

"I don't know what—" she stopped talking.

"What? What's wrong?" I asked, freaking out a little because I couldn't see anything very clearly.

"We're going downstairs. Hold on to me."

I followed Daphne down the stairs. It was much cooler and had a faint musty smell. The room was suddenly flooded with light and I had to blink several times to allow my eyes to adjust.

"Wow," Daphne and I both said at the same time.

We were in a large basement filled with what looked like a full kitchen, several couches and chairs along with a dining room table and more chairs.

"What is this?" I asked aloud.

"This is our meeting place," Magnolia said. "Make yourselves comfortable."

Daphne and I looked at each other, both of us clearly stunned.

"Your meeting place?" I asked.

"Yes. Our coven meets here. Always has," Coral said with a smile. "That's why you saw us on those tapes."

I looked away, embarrassment flooding my face. It wasn't as if my mother hadn't told me that. Yet, I'd let my imagination run wild with why they might've been in the factory at night.

"Let's get started everyone. Daphne, Violet, welcome to our lovely clubhouse!" my mom said, walking to the seating area and sitting down in one of the chairs.

Daphne and I sat next to each other on one of the couches.

"Okay, I know you two have a lot of questions. We can't answer everything tonight, but we can explain what happened. Hopefully, that will put your mind at ease about us, Violet," my mother said, looking directly at me.

I nodded my head, still on edge, but willing to hear what they had to say.

"Lila, why don't you tell the girls what happened?" Magnolia asked, taking a seat in one of the purple over-stuffed chairs.

Lila looked nervous, but stood in the center of the area and began to talk.

"It was an accident," she began. "Dale's death was an accident," she reiterated.

My mouth dropped open as I expected her to tell us she accidentally killed the man. I couldn't believe sweet Lila could hurt anyone. I instantly felt guilty for turning over the tapes. Lila didn't belong in prison!

"What happened?" I asked, anxious to know the story, but scared at the same time.

She took a deep breath. "I was hiding out in one of the upstairs offices, keeping an eye on those men. We didn't want them to find our secret room and had been taking shifts to watch them. One night, I was sitting in the dark room when I saw the man, Dale, walk by. Once he went past me, I stood inside the doorway, watching him skulk about. That's when it happened!" She buried her face in her hands and stopped talking.

"What?" Daphne and I asked at the same time.

Coral got up from her seat and put a hand on Lila's shoulder. "It's okay, hon. Tell them the rest."

Lila wiped her eyes and took a deep breath before telling us the rest. "He opened the door to a laundry chute. It had been closed up for a reason. It was a safety hazard. I saw him reach in like he was looking for something and knew I had to warn him. I stepped out of the office in time to see him reach too far and fall down the laundry chute."

I gasped, covering my mouth with my hand as it all became clear to me.

"I screamed and raced to the chute, calling out for him," she continued, sorrow in her voice. "I didn't hear anything and feared the worst. I raced down to the second floor where I knew the chute opened into. I yanked open the door and there he was," she murmured. "He was already dead. I pulled him out, hoping there would be something I could do, but it was too late."

"Oh, Lila," I whispered.

She gave me a watery smile. "It was horrible. I'm assuming he broke his neck and was killed instantly."

"Why didn't you tell the sheriff what happened?" I asked her. "Why so much secrecy?"

Lila looked at her friends and shrugged her shoulders. "I don't know."

"Where was his partner?" Daphne asked.

"He wasn't there that night. It was just Dale. We didn't trust the man. He was very shady," Lila said, regaining her composure. "Something felt off about him. We all felt it, which was why we decided to keep an eye on things here."

"If his neck was broken and his body was found outside the laundry chute, why wouldn't Harold declare it an accident?" I asked. "Why all the drama?"

"We don't know," Magnolia answered.

I looked at each of them and could see how stressed they all were. I understood why they didn't immediately go to the police, but now it seemed like it was time.

"Don't you think it's riskier to allow Harold to keep investigating rather than simply telling him you saw the accident?"

"We've thought about that, but how do we explain Lila's presence that night?" my mom asked.

I didn't know, but the truth would set them free. Continuing to lie and harbor their secret would only embroil them further in the investigation. I had to make them see reason.

# CHAPTER 17

By the time I made it home, it was close to four in the morning, my usual time for getting up. Despite being up nearly twenty-four hours, I wasn't really tired. I was too energized by what I had learned. My mother was innocent. Her friends were innocent. I didn't have to feel guilty or worry the sheriff would haul them off to jail.

I considered staying up for a bit, but knew I would regret it later. I could go to bed now and get a few hours of sleep. I wasn't going home today, but there was no reason I couldn't leave tomorrow. Nothing was keeping me in Lemon Bliss. Not anymore. My mom would be okay and I didn't have to worry about whether Gabriel was willing to work out a long-distance relationship. That minor detail had taken care of itself. There was no relationship. Not surprising at all.

I crashed once I crawled under the covers. With the adrenaline fading, I fell right to sleep.

When I woke, it was after nine. It had been a long time since I had been in bed that late. Even though I hadn't had a lot of sleep, I felt refreshed. The truth had certainly set me free. I hoped it had made all of them feel better.

I made my way downstairs and started some coffee before checking my phone for messages. Nothing. I couldn't deny it hurt a little. I had hoped to find something from Gabriel, but nothing. While holding my phone, it started to ring. My mother's face appeared on the screen.

"Hello, mom."

"Violet, I'm sorry, did I wake you?"

"No, I was up. What's up?"

"I'd like to stop by. Are you available in say thirty minutes?"

"Yes, that's fine. I'll see you then."

I hung up and raced back upstairs to take a quick shower. By the time I was toweled off and dressed, I could hear my mother downstairs.

"Violet! Are you here?"

"Be right down," I hollered, slipping on a pair of sandals.

She was walking around the room, running her hand over the trinkets left behind by my grandmother.

"Oh, there you are. You look beautiful, dear."

I ran a hand over my wet hair. "Thanks. What brings you by?"

"Well now that we've cleared the air, I wanted to talk with you more about who you are," she said with a genuine smile.

I shrugged a shoulder. "Okay, I'm ready to listen."

"Sit," she said, taking a seat on the couch.

I took my seat and stared at her. I had a million questions but I couldn't seem to form even one.

"Ask me anything."

"I don't really know what to ask. I mean, I guess, what exactly are my powers?"

As I heard my question, I couldn't help my internal eye

roll. This was nuts, but then here I was, thinking I was a witch. All because my quirky mother told me so.

"Well, I think we've already determined you have the gift of premonition. You have the magic within you, which means you can cast spells," she explained.

"How do I know what a spell is? I mean if I say 'abracadabra' what happens?"

She chuckled and shook her head. "Not quite. Spells are usually passed down or written with a specific purpose in mind. Lila is really good at writing spells. When we need something, we usually rely on her."

"Why would you need to write a spell?"

"Oh, for a number of different reasons. It's hard to go into all that. It's more of something you learn by seeing and doing, not by telling."

I nodded my head, still not really understanding. "What are your powers?"

"I'm a lot like your grandmother. I have a knack for charming things."

"What do you mean like grandma?" I asked, suddenly very curious. I remembered my grandmother was a master baker. Was that the result of witchcraft?

She smiled and looked wistful. "The flowers outside. That was her. She charmed them. She loved flowers and hated when they wilted. It always made her so sad, so she used her magic to make them bountiful. That was why her lemon trees were so fruitful. She never had to worry about how much rain we got or the weather."

"Wow. I wondered why they were so bright and beautiful."

"You'll have that ability as well, I suspect. The family has all been proficient in charming things, including people, which is why you must be careful. I should have told you before this, but I didn't want to freak you out."

A sudden thought occurred. "What about Gabriel? Did I charm him?"

"No, you would know if you charmed a man to fall in love with you. Trust me," she said with obvious experience.

"Tell me!" I giggled, wanting to hear how she charmed a man.

She rolled her eyes as she shook her head. "It was horrible. Thankfully, I had my own mother to tell me what happened and how to fix it. When you have charmed a man to fall in love with you, it is all in. The man will not be able to live without you. It isn't pretty."

"I feel like I'm way behind the ball on this. Do I need to learn it all? I mean, I don't plan on practicing witchcraft or casting spells or anything like that. I've been okay this long, I don't think I need to learn now," I said.

She wrung her hands and I could tell something had her concerned. "Violet, it isn't that simple. Witches tend to come into their full powers around your age. It's dangerous for you to remain ignorant to your gift. I would like to teach you and help guide you through this process."

The thought I could actually be a danger to society had never occurred to me. "Really? Are you saying I could wave a hand and cause something to blow up?"

"Maybe not blow up, but you will likely be able to move things without physically touching them. It's part of being a witch. We must be very cautious with our powers. Sometimes, thinking about something you want can make it appear. There's a trick to turning off that gift. Please say you'll stay in Lemon Bliss and let me show you how to use your gifts," she said, reaching out and taking my hand.

"Oh Mom, I don't know about that. Do all witches have the same gifts or powers?" I asked.

"Sometimes, but usually every witch is a little different," she explained.

I nodded, still not really understanding everything. "Like what? What other magical powers might I have?"

She threw her hands wide. "Oh my, the possibilities are endless. Most witches can heal people with their powers, but some rely on spells. Summoning the dead or speaking to the dead is also a fairly common. My mother spoke with animals. Being a witch means you are more in-tuned to your senses. You are a part of the earth. We get our strength from the earth and the rest of the elements. Oh, Violet, there is so much information. I can't possibly tell you everything in one sitting," she said with exasperation.

"It's okay. Is there a book or something I can read?" I asked, feeling more than a little overwhelmed.

"No!" she burst out. "Don't read any books. They will fill your head with nonsense."

"Mom, there has to be a way for me to do my own research."

She patted my hand and stood up. "I know it's a lot, but because it's such a dangerous secret, we can't exactly put it into books. The risk of our secrets being uncovered because someone accidentally left a book in the wrong place is too great."

I ran my hands through my wet hair. "Mom, don't you have a book of spells or something like that?"

She shrugged a shoulder, telling me all I needed to know.

"Can I read it?"

She started laughing. "I don't think you would know what you were reading. The book is old, very old. It dates back more than a few centuries. It is more of a guide than a how-to. It's tucked away, nice and safe. When you're ready, I'll show you."

"It's in the factory, isn't it?"

She grinned and winked, but didn't answer.

"That's why you guys went to such great lengths to keep Dale and George away from your secret."

Another shrug of her shoulder.

"Wow, I feel like I just got dropped into calculus. I have no clue where to even start," I muttered.

"I understand that. I really do. I feel terrible for not teaching you all of this over the years, but I was scared. We all were. I would so love to have you back home. Let me make up for lost time. Daphne will be living here again. Magnolia will be showing her the ropes. We want you to join the coven, be a part of our family."

"Can I think about it?" I asked softly.

"Of course. Take some time, I'll be here."

"Thank you, Mom. I promise I'll think about it. There's just a lot to consider, and I can't seem to get my head wrapped around everything."

She paused at the door and looked at me. "What happened between you and Gabriel? Coral wouldn't give me the whole story, but I gathered you guys had some kind of disagreement."

I sighed, debating how much to tell her, and then just dumped it out. When I finished telling her why Gabriel and I argued, she was smiling.

"What?" I asked, wondering why she looked so delighted.

"You two are perfect for each other. You need a partner who can serve as your other half. A checks and balances kind of thing. Don't be too hard on him. He was looking out for us."

I took a little offense to that. "I wasn't trying to get any of you in trouble. I tried to look out for you all as well."

"He knows about witches and isn't afraid of them. That's not easy to find, trust me. Shoot, trust all of us," she mumbled. "A man like Gabriel doesn't come along very often. Can I tell you a secret?"

"What?" I muttered.

"You're not the only one with premonitions and the ability to predict the future."

I laughed. "What are you trying to say?"

"I'm saying the man is worth a little forgiveness and compromise," she said, that warm smile spreading across her face.

"I don't know. Maybe I'll try calling him later," I told her.

"Good, you should. Goodbye, dear."

"Bye, Mom."

I followed her out on the porch. Everything looked different, like I was seeing the world with an entirely new perspective. The sun felt warmer, the air fresher and I could hear the leaves of one of the oak trees in the yard rustling with the breeze. I felt different somehow.

Wanting to really see the flowers my grandmother had a hand in creating, I stood there, taking in the huge blossoms and vivid colors. They were amazing. It felt like I was seeing her. I wondered if her spirit truly was at the house, with me, surrounding me. That was one power I wanted to tap into. I missed my grandma so much. I wanted to talk with her. I didn't know how any of this worked, but I was hoping it was a lot like having a phone conversation.

I grinned, realizing the blooms weren't the work of any gardener. This was magic, and I liked this kind of magic. I started to think about how I could use magic in my own life, but quickly dismissed the thought. I couldn't use it to better my life. My life was pretty good already, and I didn't want to risk some horrible consequences as the result of using magic for personal gain.

Checking my watch, I saw that it would be rush hour at the bakery. I didn't want to call and stress Tara out. I'd wait. I was going to go home Monday. My mind was made up. Whether I stayed in Lemon Bliss was yet to be determined.

# CHAPTER 18

The following day, I pondered my options. The more I thought about opening a bakery here, the more inclined I was to go for it. I loved a challenge, and this would be a fun one. Plus, my curiosity about my witchy talents was growing by leaps and bounds. Every so often, I gave myself a mental shake, wondering if I'd lost my d*mn mind.

Meanwhile, I was being stubborn about calling Gabriel. I knew that, but so was he. Why hadn't he called me? My mom had me convinced Gabriel was worth trying for, but if he was through with me, I wasn't going to grovel. I did have some pride.

My phone rang. Glancing at the screen, I was disappointed to see it wasn't him. Instead, it was my mom. "Hi, Mom, what's up?" I asked, looking at the clock and realizing she hadn't left all that long ago.

"Lila is speaking to the sheriff right now," she blurted out. I could hear the worry in her voice, which made me quite worried as well. Nothing rattled my mom. This had to be serious.

"She is?" I asked in surprise.

"Yes, after our meeting last night, we felt it was best if she explained to Harold what she saw. Hopefully, this will end the investigation and he will leave all of us alone. It should also mean he won't need you to stay around. I want you to be free to make your own choices. Much as I'd love to have you here, I don't want you to feel pressured."

"Oh," I said, suddenly a little let down to be given a free pass to leave Lemon Bliss. It was nice having the excuse, even if I enjoyed complaining about it a bit.

"Does that mean you'll be leaving right away?" she asked, hesitantly.

"I'll be heading back on Monday morning. I'll let you know if I decide to come back," I promised her. "I need to talk with Tara and get her take on all of this. My decision will affect her life as well."

"I'll stop by tomorrow," she said and hung up. "Don't leave without saying goodbye, please?"

I could hear the strain in her voice and knew that she, along with her friends, must be very worried. Lila could be in a great deal of trouble. I hoped Harold would go easy on her, but he had to answer to someone as well. He may have to charge her with a crime to cover his own butt.

"What a mess," I groaned.

I sat back down and started to put together a business plan. It was something I knew I would have to have should I decide to apply for a loan for a new bakery. It would also give me a better idea about the numbers and likelihood of being success-ful. In the back of my mind, I couldn't quiet a little voice that kept telling me this was the right thing to do. Lemon Bliss had gone from feeling like the past I'd left behind to destiny. Which was a little wacky. All those days in the kitchen with Grandma were training me for my future as a baker in her little town.

By the time I had finished the plan, I was feeling more

confident and more convinced I was making the right decision. My stomach was a jumble of nerves as I considered the big change. I could feasibly keep my current bakery and let Tara run it. I would need to hire more staff to make up for my absence and give her a fat raise, of course. I needed to talk with Tara. First, I needed to fortify my nerves and resolve with food. An iced mocha sounded like just what I needed.

Sliding on my shoes, I grabbed my purse and prepared to run down to the Crooked Coffee for a boost of energy.

When I yanked open the door to leave, I got quite the surprise. I yelped and jumped back.

"Harold, I mean, Sheriff Smith," I managed to get out, suddenly very nervous.

"Good afternoon, Violet. Can we talk?"

I looked around the living room and didn't see anything incriminating. "Sure, come in, please."

"Were you on your way out?" he asked, looking at the purse in my hand.

"Yes, just a coffee run, though. It can wait."

"Good."

He sat down on the couch and waited for me to take a seat as well.

"What did you need?" I asked, unsure why he would need to talk with me. If Lila had filled him in, the case should be closed. At least in my mind it was.

"I guess you probably know that Lila came to talk with me," he started.

I nodded my head. "Yes, my mother told me."

"Do you believe her story?" he asked, looking me straight in the eye.

I gulped down the lump in my throat before I schooled my features to calm. I didn't want to give the impression I was nervous, but I was failing miserably. "I think so, yes. I'm not sure I know all the details. I didn't think it was any of my business."

He stared at me in a way that made me feel as if he was peeling back layers of my brain, one at a time and reading my thoughts.

"Well, I'm not convinced," he said, nearly making me choke.

"Uh, why not, if I may ask? From what I understand, she witnessed the man's accident, and tried to help him. The accident took his life, and it was too late to help. Isn't that what she told you?"

"It is, but something isn't adding up."

I shrugged a shoulder. "I'm not sure I can help you. I wasn't there. But I believe her story."

"I'm sure you do, but tell me this, why didn't she just tell me? Why didn't she call for help? Lila left a man dead in that factory and went home to bed as if nothing happened. Doesn't that strike you as odd?" he pried.

Now he was making me very nervous. This was a different Harold. The Harold I had grown up with was more laid back and accepting. He had always liked Lila and the rest of the ladies. Now, I got the impression he was not quite as fond of them as he once was. That could be very bad for the coven. For me as well, if I chose to move back to Lemon Bliss.

"Maybe she was in shock?" I offered. "I'm sure she was horrified by what she witnessed. People do strange things when they're in shock."

"Possibly. She didn't tell you why she was there in the middle of the night?"

I smiled. "Who knows why Lila does half the things she does? I certainly don't. It's just Lila," I said with a tight smile.

He didn't smile back, "Lila is going to find herself in real trouble one of these days. She said she was curious about what the investigators were doing, and wanted to see for herself if there were any ghosts in the building."

I grabbed onto that explanation with both hands. "That sounds like Lila. I'm sure it was all very exciting to have real-life supernatural investigators right here in Lemon Bliss."

Harold wiped his hands on his pants, before glancing around the living room. "This place looks just the way your grandmother left it."

I smiled and looked around. "Yes, it does."

"You moving back?" he asked.

I wasn't sure I wanted him to know my plans. I certainly didn't want to be on his radar. If I were going to start learning witchcraft, I would probably make a lot of mistakes. I didn't want to risk exposing us all by doing something while under his close watch.

"I haven't decided yet," I answered truthfully. "I'm tossing around the idea."

He eyed me with more scrutiny than I would have liked. "Well, in the meantime, as the property owner, you need to secure that factory. I don't want another mishap like that again. There is still a chance you could be held liable for the man's death."

My mouth dropped open. "Excuse me? He was breaking and entering. The entire town knew it, but no one stopped them, including you, Sheriff Smith."

That seemed to take some of the wind out of his sails. "That's not the point. The place needs better locks, and I would suggest boarding up that laundry chute, just in case anyone else gets any ideas. Once people in the county hear about what happened, they're all going to be curious. We're going to be flooded with ghost chasers trying to find something."

I took a deep breath, not wanting to argue or push the issue. I couldn't afford to. "I'll do what I can sheriff.

However, I would also like to request that you use your law enforcement capabilities to remove trespassers, instead of letting them take up residence in my factory."

"Are you asking me to patrol that area?"

"No. I'm asking you do something if you know there are supernatural investigators hanging out in the factory and installing surveillance cameras. I have half a mind to go after Mr. Cannon for trespassing and damaging private property."

He stood up, and I quickly got to my feet. I wouldn't let him intimidate me. "I'll be leaving now. You're free to leave. The investigation is closed. In fact, it might be best if you did leave town."

I raised an eyebrow at his veiled threat. "Are you suggesting I might have a problem?"

"Not at all, Miss Broussard. I'm suggesting you may want to think twice about who you align yourself with."

He walked out the door, leaving me standing in the living room shaken to the core. I had a bad feeling, and this time, I didn't need to rely on my witch powers—not that I knew how to do that yet—to know what it meant. Sheriff Smith had all but dropped a gauntlet on my family. Whatever Lila said had only increased his suspicion instead of allaying it. I needed to call and warn my mother.

I dug in my purse and pulled out my phone.

"Mom?"

"Yes, what's wrong?" she asked, obviously hearing the tension in my voice.

"Harold was just here. I don't think he's buying Lila's story," I blurted out.

"Oh no," she muttered. "What did he say?"

I took a few deep breaths to calm my nerves before relaying what had been said. "Do you think he's going to do anything?"

"I don't know, but we'll have to be much more careful.

Harold had always turned a blind eye in the past, but I have a feeling that's about to change."

"What about the factory? The meeting place? What if he finds it?"

"Violet, that place has been around for over a hundred years and no one has found it yet. Before the factory was built, there was another building there where we met in the very same location. The door is charmed. No one can see it. If someone happened to stumble upon it, there are other spells in place to hide it."

I breathed a sigh of relief. It explained why the investigators never found the door. I had watched the tapes and been in the factory and never saw it either.

"Okay. He wants me to lock the place up tight. I'll make sure to give you a key," I said, trying to think of where I could find a padlock in Lemon Bliss.

She giggled, "You can put twenty padlocks on it. I won't need any keys, dear."

"Oh, duh, sorry, I forgot," I said, feeling foolish.

"It's okay, dear. Relax. Why don't you go get that coffee you were going to get before Harold stopped you?"

"I'm going to. Wait, how did you know?"

Another soft laugh before the line went dead.

This was going to be very weird. I wondered if it had been like that my entire life. Those times I hadn't wanted to talk to her on the phone and made up excuses to get off, or the many excuses I used to avoid coming home—had she known I was lying?

I brushed away the feeling of guilt and regret about lying to my mother. That was in the past. I would be much more careful from this day forward. Now that I knew my mother had more than a sixth sense or motherly intuition, I would have to choose my words more carefully.

Grabbing my purse, I headed out the door, making sure to lock it behind me. I didn't usually bother, but now I felt as if I were being watched. I drove to Crooked Coffee and headed inside. The place was relatively quiet in the middle of the day, except for one table.

*Crap.* I should have looked to see who was inside before I came in. At that moment, Gabriel turned around and saw me.

# CHAPTER 19

*I* froze in my steps. I couldn't move as he looked at me. Briefly, I wondered if I could use my power to cloak myself. Maybe, if I thought real hard, he wouldn't see me and I could walk right back out the door and pretend it never happened.

*Too late.* He rose from his seat at our usual table and walked towards me. "Hi."

"Hi," I squeaked out.

"Afternoon fix?" he asked, with a smile.

"Yup."

I walked up to the counter, leaving Gabriel standing there. I didn't know what to say to him. Half of me wanted to say I was sorry, and the other half was still angry that he'd gotten mad at me in the first place. I needed coffee. That was my only goal at that moment.

Coffee first, and then I'd deal with Gabriel. Armed with an ice-cold mocha, I turned around, ready to face the man who had me twisted in knots.

He was still standing there, watching and waiting. I felt as if he could see right through me.

"Have dinner with me," he said in a low voice.

"Gabriel," I started.

He shook his head, stopping my protest. "I want to talk. Please?"

How could I deny him? I wanted to talk as well. I needed to try and explain myself a little better. Maybe this time he would be willing to listen. "Okay."

"I can make us dinner. That way we don't have to worry about being disturbed, or have any busy bodies getting in the way. This is about me and you, not my aunt or your mother," he said, putting one of his hands on my elbow.

I nodded, feeling as if he was casting a spell over me. I wondered if he truly was a man witch. Did those exist? They had to. I had a feeling that many things I had always chalked up to fairytales might actually exist after all. My world had changed, and I needed to be prepared to be a bit more accepting.

"Dinner at your place or mine?" I asked.

He shrugged, "Which do you prefer? I'll warn you that I live in a small house with an even smaller kitchen."

I laughed, "My place it is. Grams would love someone using that big kitchen of hers to make a real meal instead of the microwave meals I've been eating."

"Perfect. I'm done with work for the day. I'll go to the store and be there in about an hour. Does that work for you?"

"Yes. Can I pick anything up?"

"Nope. I got it. This is me treating you to dinner. All you have to do is kick back and keep me company while I mess up your kitchen."

"Sounds like a date," I smiled, and headed out the door with a bounce in my step that had nothing to do with the coffee in my hand.

I drove straight back to the house and tidied up a bit. I called Tara and reconfirmed my promise to her that I would be home on Monday and that we needed to talk. Next, I called my mother. I didn't want any surprise visitors. Hopefully, she would pass along the message and the ladies would give Gabriel and I some privacy for once. They had meddled enough. It was up to us to decide what was best for us, without them pushing us towards each other.

I freshened up, lit a few scented candles Grams had left behind, and waited for Gabriel to show. He arrived, carrying several bags.

"I thought you said you were making dinner. This looks like a feast for a week!"

"A good chef is always prepared. I didn't know what you had in the cupboards, so I made sure to bring everything I might need."

I followed him into the kitchen and watched as he put the bags down and started unpacking ingredients.

"What are you making?" I asked.

He looked at me, winked and grinned. "It's a surprise."

"Oh, that sounds intriguing. Can I help?"

"Nope. I want you to sit right there and keep me company. Here, you can open this," he said, pulling out a bottle of wine.

I smiled, taking the bottle and opening it, before pouring two glasses. I sat down on one of the stools and watched him work.

"Coconut shrimp?" I asked, after checking out the ingredients spread across the large center island.

He grinned, "If you're in Louisiana, you're eating shrimp."

Laughing, I nodded my head. "So true."

Watching him clean the shrimp, I settled on a stool by the counter. It was nice to have him in the kitchen. In the house, really. I tended to spend a lot of time alone, if only because I was busy running my bakery. Oh, I had friends, but I lived alone. This big old house was a lot of space to bang around in all by myself. Having Gabriel here made the space warmer and friendlier, more the way it felt when Grams was alive.

"So, ready to address the elephant in the room?" he asked, measuring rice out of the bag.

"I suppose we should get that out of the way, just in case you want to pack up your shrimp and leave."

He shook his head. "Nope, and I won't. I already know that as much as I know I love cake."

I burst out laughing. "What?"

He grinned. "Nothing. Sorry, it's a saying I heard. I do love cake though, so it works."

"It's cute. I wanted to apologize. I mean, I still feel I did the right thing, but I can understand why you were upset by it. I should have told you," I said, softly.

He shook his head, "No, you didn't need to. I'm sorry I got so mad. I'm protective of Aunt Coral. I've worried someone would find out about her, and think she deserved to be prosecuted simply because she was charmed. It terrifies me to think about her being taken away," he explained.

"That's sweet. I love how protective you are of her."

He stopped what he was doing and walked towards me. I put my glass of wine down, not sure what he was going to do. Placing his hands on either side of my face, he looked into my eyes before kissing me. His kiss was quick, but hot. Pleasure zinged through me, leaving me slightly startled and befuddled. I hadn't expected that kiss.

"I'll protect you, too," he said gently.

"What?"

He smiled and went back to making dinner. "I said I'll protect you as well. All of you."

I wasn't sure what he meant, but didn't want to inadvertently say something that would give us all away. I still wasn't quite sure if he knew the whole lot of Coral's friends were witches, along with me. I was still getting used to that zany idea myself.

"Thank you."

He chuckled. "You don't have to hide your secret from me, Violet. I already know. I've known about your mother for a long time. Unlike the women here in Lemon Bliss, my mother was far more open about witches and the supernatural world. When I came here, it didn't take me long to figure out who was who. Please don't think you have to hide that part of you from me."

My mouth was hanging open and I knew I must look foolish, but I couldn't speak. "You know?"

"Yes, I know and I'm okay with it."

"Wow."

"Can you find me a big pot?" he asked, as if we had been talking about nothing more important than the weather.

I slid off the stool and started opening cupboards until I found one. "I only just found out myself."

"I know."

"What! You knew that too?"

"Aunt Coral explained they had to keep their secret very close. It wasn't until the death investigation began that they realized they had to tell you. I'm glad they did. You're going to make a great witch," he grinned.

I started laughing. That had to be the most ridiculous thing I'd ever heard. "Hopefully I don't turn anyone into toads or blow anything up while I go through this learning curve my Mom promised me. I'm still not quite used to the idea myself."

"I'll make sure not to make you mad."

"I can't believe you've known this whole time and never said anything."

He shrugged a shoulder. "What was I supposed to say? It doesn't change anything."

"Good. I'm glad you're so okay with all of this. I think you took it better than I did."

He allowed me to help him a little. Together we made coconut shrimp and fried rice. It smelled so good I wanted to dive in. I managed to mind my manners and set the table. We sat down and enjoyed our meal. It was a absolutely delicious, and Gabriel was downright charming. Plus, the man could cook.

"I hear you're tossing around the idea of moving here," he said, wiping his mouth with a napkin.

"I'm thinking about it. I need to work some things out before I can just up and move," I explained. "I don't know why my mother and the other ladies can't understand that."

"Of course you do. I think they do understand it by the way, but they don't care. They just want you here. So do I."

He stood and began to clear the table, but I ordered him into the living room. "You cooked, I'll clean up. Please, sit a minute, relax, put your feet up, and I'll be right there."

He didn't put up much of a fight. I quickly cleared the table and rinsed the dishes, leaving them in the sink to deal with tomorrow. Thankfully, Gabriel was a tidy cook and didn't leave a mess. I had to admit he had a number of major points in his favor. I had yet to find many marks against him. Even the small mark after our fight had been erased. I now understood why he had been upset.

I refilled the glasses with wine and carried them into the living room.

"I suppose you heard about Lila's confession?" I asked, sitting down beside him on the couch.

"I did. I guess that means it's all over now?"

Letting out a long breath, I replied. "I hope so. Harold came by earlier, and he was kind of a jerk. I have a feeling we are all going to be watched very closely. He all but told me not to come back."

"Don't worry about Harold. He doesn't have a clue what

goes on around here. He just wants to feel important. I think he's had a crush on Lila for years. The fact she didn't tell him what happened had to have stung a little, too. He'll get over it and forget all about this supernatural investigator stuff soon enough."

"I hope so. If I'm going to start a new life here, the last thing I want is the sheriff breathing down my neck. I'm too new at this and I know I will make mistakes. I don't want to end up blowing everyone's cover."

"You'll do fine," he said, wrapping an arm around my shoulders and squeezing me in close.

I rested against his side for a few minutes, enjoying his clean, masculine scent and his warmth and strength. I thought about what it would be like to see him more than temporarily. I could certainly get used to it.

"Do you work tomorrow?" I asked, fighting back a yawn. The wine and full belly combined with my lack of sleep the night before were making me very sleepy.

"Nope. I don't usually work on Sundays."

I took a deep breath, gathering my courage. "Would you like to stay?" I whispered.

His arm tightened around me. "I'd love to."

I let out the breath I had been holding, relieved he hadn't rejected me. I had no idea what I was doing with him, but I was ready to give it a try. What's the worst that could happen? Oh right, a broken heart. I'm sure there was a spell to fix that.

# CHAPTER 20

"Will I see you before you leave?" Gabriel asked as he stood by the front door the following day.

"I'm going to go by and see my mom and then I'll probably take off. The sooner I get back and start figuring out how I can run two bakeries, the sooner I can come back here," I said, wrapping my arms around his neck.

"Okay. Call me tonight and let me know how things go. If you can't swing it, don't worry about it. We'll figure something out," he said, before kissing me and walking out the door.

I stepped out on the porch and inhaled the heavy perfume from the hundreds of blossoms. It was a smell I could certainly grow to love. It was heady and a little powerful, but it had a way of lifting the spirits. I looked at the rows of lavender and decided they were the reason for my fabulous mood. Well, there was that and Gabriel.

After a quick shower, I stripped the bed and made a mental note to have a new washer and dryer delivered. For that, I would use my inheritance. It was for grandma's house after all. Grabbing the perishables from the fridge, I put them in a bag to take to my mother. If it took me longer than I hoped to wrap things up, I didn't want to come home to a fridge full of spoiled food. I took one last look around the house and smiled.

"I'll be back, Grams," I said with a smile.

A cold breeze brushed over my arms. I had a feeling I was going to have to get used to that if I lived in the house. I would ask my mom, but I was sure that was the spirit my mother had referred to before.

After locking up, I paused in the yard and glanced around. The faint scent of lemon drifted to me. Spinning around, I looked to the abandoned lemon orchards in the distance behind the house. Even after Grams closed up the lemon tea business, she tended to those orchards. Although now that I reconsidered, it occurred to me she probably didn't do too much work. She likely cast a few spells to make the lemon trees happy.

With a wistful smile, I turned away and headed to my mother's house. I never did understand why she hadn't just moved into my grandmother's house. It made more sense it would be passed to her, rather than me. I already knew what she would say if I asked her. She'd always made it clear that she believed the house was part of my destiny.

"Mom?" I said, knocking on the door before pushing it open.

"I'm in here," she called out from the kitchen.

I walked into the kitchen to see her at the table with Lila, Magnolia and Coral. I was instantly embarrassed. They all knew, I could see it. The knowing smiles on their faces were further confirmation.

"How was your night, dear?" Coral cooed in a high falsetto.

"Leave her alone," Magnolia scolded.

I knew there was a reason I'd always liked her the best.

"My night was fine, thank you," I replied.

"What's that?" my mom asked, pointing to the bag.

"Stuff from my fridge. I didn't want it to spoil."

"You're leaving?" Lila asked, shock in her voice.

I nodded my head. "Yes. I have to. This was a nice visit, but I need to get back to my life. Before I make any decisions, I need to figure out what I'm doing with my bakery."

Magnolia smiled. "We're so glad you came, dear. You've discovered your true calling. *That* is a very big deal."

She had a point. "You're right. I am very happy to have learned the truth, and I do look forward to learning more, but life calls. I'll see you ladies soon, I hope."

"I'll walk you out," Mom said, following me to the door.

She followed me back outside, pausing beside my car with me. "I know it's a big decision, but just know I will support you in whatever you decide. Even if it takes you several months or longer to get things situated, I'll be here. I can't wait to share this journey with you," she said, hugging me tight.

"I know, Mom. I know I'll be back, I just don't know when."

She nodded and winked, "But, you will be back. I'm glad you can admit that to yourself."

I laughed as I climbed into my car. Waving goodbye, I headed towards the Crooked Coffee to get my fix before I hit the road. I was going to miss the little place. It was nice not having to wait in line to grab a quick cup of coffee. It was definitely one of the perks of small town living.

"You're leaving, aren't you?" Daphne stopped me when I got out of my car.

"Daphne, I have to."

She was shaking her head. "No, no, no. I have to talk to you. Are you going in to get coffee?"

"Yes."

"Great. I'll get some and we can sit down and chat before

you go. You have to know there is no way I'm letting you get away that easy."

I giggled. "As long as you don't bust out handcuffs, I'm okay with you holding me here for a bit longer, but then I have to get going. I have a long drive home."

"*This* is your home. You're going back to that other place to pack, but this is where you belong," she corrected me.

I didn't argue with her. We ordered our coffees and sat down. I could tell she had something to tell me. She was practically oozing with excitement.

"Lay it on me. What'd you do?"

She clapped her hands. "It isn't what I did. It's what we're going to do!"

"What are we going to do, Daphne?" I asked, feeling I should humor the girl who was clearly very excited about her news.

"I got the loan!"

My mind spun trying to replay our previous conversations and find the missing piece of the puzzle. "What loan?" I asked, when I realized I had no idea what she was talking about.

"Our loan! For the bakery we're going to open!" she practically shouted.

I glanced around and noticed several people staring at us. "Daphne, I didn't say I was ready to make that step."

She waved away my words. "No, you didn't, but you didn't have to. I know you too well. I went and had a meeting with the manager at my bank. He gave me preliminary approval for the loan. Of course, we'll need collateral and we'll both need to sign, but he's on board. It was strange, like a little too easy," she said, rubbing her chin in deep thought.

My eyes widened. "Did you charm him?" I hissed.

"What? Charm him. What do you mean? I am charming and most men do find me attractive, but if you're implying I flirted with him to get the loan, no. I'm not quite that desperate, Violet. Sheesh, give me some credit."

I rolled my eyes. "Not like that. I mean *charmed*," I said, emphasizing out the word.

I looked into her clueless eyes. Clearly, Magnolia hadn't gotten that far in her witch training with Daphne.

"Violet, really, what are you talking about?"

I leaned forward and lowered my voice to a whisper. "Charming is something witches do. You can charm a person to do what you want."

Her eyes bugged out and her mouth fell open. She slapped a hand over her mouth and shook her head. "Oh my, what if I did? I didn't mean to, but it was a little too easy."

I started giggling. "Oh well. It isn't like I'm not good for the money, and it was an innocent accident. I think as long as we are responsible and make our payments on time, there isn't anything truly wrong with it. I hope so anyway. I don't want there to be some horrible repercussions for using our magic for personal gain. We really need to talk to our moms about this stuff."

"I can't believe I did that. How come my charms weren't enough to keep my husband faithful?" she grumbled.

"I think you should count yourself lucky you found out his true character before you had children with him."

She nodded and took a drink of her coffee. "That's true. Okay, so does that mean you're ready to do this?" she asked with a wide grin, her eyes pleading.

I let out a long breath. "I am, but I have to figure out what to do with my other store. And, we still need to find a place for the bakery. It will take months or more to get the necessary equipment, get the wiring done that will be needed to run it, and so on. Starting a business takes a lot of work."

She looked down at her coffee cup. "Well, I happen to

know a handyman that will probably jump at the chance to take care of a lot of that stuff."

"Oh no. You heard, too?"

She started giggling. "I went by your house this morning to tell you about the loan. I saw his truck in the driveway and figured I better keep on going."

I put a hand to my forehead, "Well, that's embarrassing."

"No, it's not. You're both single, and he's totally into you. I think it's cute and I'm very excited to get some free work, or at least steeply discounted work around the bakery."

"We need to contact a realtor and see if there are any commercial properties available," I said, quickly changing the subject.

"Done."

"What? Dang, you move fast."

"Want to see it before you leave?" she said, dangling a set of keys in front of me.

"You already have keys?" I said, in astonishment. "Did you charm that person, too?"

She chuckled, "No, I just know the guy who owns the building. I asked if I could check it out and he gave me the keys. I'm giving them back tomorrow. The realtor thinks this place will be perfect, but I haven't seen it yet. Come on, let's go see it. It won't take long."

I checked my watch. "Fine, but I can't stay long. I want to get on the road so I don't hit the weekend traffic out of New Orleans."

She squealed and jumped up from the table. I followed behind her in my car. When she pulled up in front of the building that was once a convenience store, I was immediately unsure. It would take a lot of work to transform the place into a bakery. I doubted a loan would cover the operating costs along with the labor and equipment, which meant Grandma's money would be getting put to use.

"Don't let the outside fool you," she said, unlocking the door and pushing it open.

I took a look around at the broken shelves littering the area along with a lot of dirt and debris. "What about the inside?" I mumbled.

"This is easy. A big dumpster and a little elbow grease, and soon this will all be good as new. Look, we could have the counter there with some little tables dotting this area. Think pink. Isn't pink a good color for a bakery?" she asked.

"Uh, I don't know. Let's go look at the back-room area," I said, walking behind the small existing counter.

I groaned. Daphne gasped.

"It's okay. We can clean this up."

"The ceiling, Daphne. There must have been a water leak or it may have been damaged in a hurricane. This could cost a lot of money to fix," I warned her.

She was smiling, "It's okay. This is it. This is our bakery. Can't you feel it? I can practically smell baking bread. Close your eyes and inhale. You can smell the yeast and sugar."

I did as she suggested and remarkably, I could smell the scents I was so familiar with in my bakery back home.

I opened my eyes and she was staring at me with tears in her eyes.

I smiled and nodded, "This is our bakery."

She screamed and grabbed me in a bear hug. I hugged her back, hoping this was the right choice.

# EPILOGUE

"**I**s this Mr. Cannon?" Harold Smith asked.

There was a long pause on the other end of the line before supernatural investigator George Cannon replied, "Yes, this is he."

"This is Sheriff Smith from Lemon Bliss. I was the one you spoke with after the death of your partner in that old lemon tea factory. I was wondering if we could get together and talk."

"Why?"

"I have some questions and I'm hoping you can answer them for me," Harold explained.

"I don't know that I have the answers you are looking for."

"Then it couldn't hurt to talk, right?" Harold pressed.

"Fine. Where?"

"Not here. Not in Lemon Bliss," the sheriff asserted. "It isn't safe here."

"Fine, Ruby Red work for you?"

"I'll be there. Can I meet you in an hour?"

"Yes."

163

Harold hung up the phone and looked around his office. He knew he was stepping in it, but those women were up to something, he just knew it. All the rumors—there had to be something to it. Those women were making him look like an idiot. Walking around like they owned the town. Enough was enough. They wouldn't make him the laughing stock of the county.

"I'll be out of the office for a few hours," he told the elderly secretary sitting at the desk outside of his own office.

He climbed into his old truck and headed out of town. He passed the old factory and stared up at the big chimney reaching into the sky. He had suspected there was something strange about that place for a long time, but had always taken the position that if they didn't bother him, he wouldn't bother them. That was over.

Lila had crossed a line. The woman had made him look like a chump. It was time to dig in and fight back.

He pulled into the diner parking lot and went inside, looking around. When he saw his target, he made a beeline for the man and slid into the booth. The waitress appeared almost instantly, delivering a glass of water and taking his order. He wasn't hungry but figured he better order a cup of coffee, at least.

As soon as the waitress walked away, he turned to face the investigator.

"What can I help you with, sheriff?"

"I want to know what's happening in that factory."

George Cannon smiled. "I was wondering how long it would take you to get on board. Those witches have been practicing magic in that factory for a long time. Dale has been researching that area for quite a while. We finally managed to convince the producers of our show to let us follow up on the lead."

"What kind of research?"

"There have been tales coming out of Lemon Bliss for centuries. Did you honestly think all those stories were based on rumors? There is a grain of truth in every rumor, Sheriff. The key is to pick it apart until you find that little nugget of truth. Once you find it, you dig in. Dale and I were on the brink of uncovering the truth before he was so unceremoniously killed," he spat with a shake of his head.

"He wasn't killed. His death was an accident. There was a witness," Harold said, keeping his cool.

George guffawed, not hiding his anger in the slightest. "Do you actually believe that? Let me guess: one of those little witches told you the story."

Harold kept his expression calm, refusing to let it show he had his own questions about whether Lila had been honest with him. "I said there was a witness. I don't need to tell you the details."

"And I don't need to tell you the details of what we uncovered in our investigation."

Harold took a deep breath, quickly considering what he should reveal. The man could have nothing; or he could hold the key to uncovering the many strange happenings in Lemon Bliss.

"Lila. Lila was spying on you guys. I have the surveillance footage from the cameras you set up. Did you get the chance to review the footage at all?"

George nodded his head. "Yes. The tapes you have are not all of the tapes. We made copies. We have more tapes with more evidence." A sly grin crossed his face. "We have the actual evidence."

"What evidence?" Harold asked, intrigued by the idea of seeing what he had long suspected.

"I wouldn't want to reveal the whole show."

"You're moving forward with the show, even after what happened to Dale?"

George shrugged a shoulder as if his friend's death was

just something that happened. That disturbed Harold, but he was more than curious to learn what they had uncovered.

"Of course, we're moving forward. Dale's death has been the best publicity we ever could have asked for. There is more interest in this episode than any we've ever had in the past. I'll be taking the lead from this point forward."

Harold stared at the man, horrified by the realization that George had gained from Dale's death and was capitalizing on it. "When will it be aired?" he asked.

"Oh, I'm still working on a few details. I want to make sure the public gets the full story. I'd hate to leave anyone hanging," George offered with a wink.

"Maybe I can help you out with those details. We can compare our evidence," Harold said, hoping to persuade the man to join forces. At this point, he wanted to be able to monitor George with his concern about George's motivations growing by the minute.

George appeared to think about the offer. "How do I know you have anything of value to add?"

"I've lived in Lemon Bliss all my life. I went to school with those women, and I've seen a lot. I haven't talked about it or made a television show about what I've seen, but that doesn't mean I don't know anything."

"I can show you some of the footage I have. Dale's notes are very interesting as well. He interviewed the ex-husband of one of them, too. That was a very interesting conversation," George explained.

Harold's face paled a bit. "He did what?"

George nodded. "Oh, you didn't know that, did you? He also tracked down the ex of a young woman named Daphne."

"Magnolia's daughter? What's she got to do with any of this? She isn't one of them," Harold countered, starting to feel uncomfortable with the direction this was going.

George shook his head slowly. "You don't know nearly as much as you think you do, Sheriff."

"Tell me," he muttered, biting back his frustration. "Who do you think they are?"

"This isn't something I can just explain. You need to see to believe. You need to have an understanding of the supernatural. If you have a closed mind, it will never make any sense to you."

"What are you saying?"

"Come back to my office in New Orleans. You couldn't possibly understand what's on the tapes if you don't understand how the supernatural works. There are signs you have to know to look for. What may appear normal to you is really anything but," he explained.

"How do I know I can trust you? What makes you such an authority figure on the subject?"

George smirked. "Haven't you seen the show?"

Harold wrinkled his nose. "As if any of that stuff is true."

"Oh, but it is. For too long, society has taught us that it's all make believe. It isn't. Supernatural beings have been forced to go underground, to hide themselves for fear of prosecution, or persecution. My job is to ferret them out. I don't want to hurt them. My viewers don't want to hurt them. We are generally curious about them. However, those women in Lemon Bliss crossed a line. We only wanted to talk to them," he said, shaking his head in what Harold believed was a feigned sadness.

Something about the man made him uneasy. He couldn't quite put his finger on it, but it was there. Thirty years in law enforcement had honed his own intuition. Gut feelings were part of the job and his gut told him this man was not who he claimed to be.

"I'd like to see what you have. Maybe I can offer you some insight to some of those stories," Harold offered, hoping to put the man at ease.

He didn't hate Lila and the others, but they had hurt him. He wanted to learn the truth, no matter what it was. If that meant befriending the man across the table from him, then that was exactly what he would do.

"Come to my office, tomorrow at two. I'll give you a sneak peek of the upcoming two-hour special. Maybe you can add some information.

Harold thought about it for a few seconds before agreeing to drive up the following day.

"I'll see you tomorrow."

"Bring any files on cases you think may be relevant. I'd love to dig up some more dirt, make it a nice, juicy episode."

Both men stood, shook hands and left the diner. As Harold drove home, he thought about some of the strange happenings that had taken place over the years. There were a few situations he definitely thought were worth investigating further. He wasn't going to take it further, not yet. For now, he would use George to get some insight. Once he could prove or disprove what he suspected, then he would decide what to do.

As he drove back into Lemon Bliss, the factory drew his attention. He hadn't released the crime scene yet and decided it couldn't hurt to take another look around. Maybe he'd find his own evidence. He didn't like George and something told him the guy wasn't completely innocent in the death of his partner. Maybe he'd have another talk with Lila. She was holding something back as well. There were far too many secrets in this town for his liking.

One layer at a time. The first layer started with the factory and whatever those supernatural investigators discovered.

\* \* \*

IF YOU'D LIKE updates when I have new releases and other

news,     sign     up     for     my     newsletter:
https://lucymayauthor.com/subscribe

For more fun with the witches in Lemon Bliss, turn the page for a sneak peek from A Spell to Tell, the next book in the Lemon Tea Series.

# EXCERPT: A SPELL TO TELL

## CHAPTER 1

"*A*re you ready for this?" I asked Daphne, taking several calming breaths.

She smiled. "Girl, I've been ready for the last three months. I didn't think this moment would ever come. I don't think I realized how much work would be involved just to get the place transformed into a bakery. I thought it would be a few ovens and sinks and then some seating in the dining room. This has been gobs of work."

Smiling, I looked around the tiny dining area of our new bakery. Today was our grand opening. I was nervous and excited at the same time.

"You've got the cash drawer in?" I asked, going through a mental checklist.

"Yes."

"Tables are cleaned, condiment bar stocked, display ready," I mumbled, as I spun around. Everything had to be just perfect.

"We're good, Violet. This is going to be great. There's already buzz around town after our soft opening last week. This is going to do fabulous! Are you ready?"

On the heels of another breath, I closed my eyes and composed myself. "Okay, I'm ready. Hit it."

She flipped the switch on the neon 'open' sign, and we were officially open for business. We both stood in the center of the dining room, staring at the front door. Daphne burst out giggling.

"I don't think there's going to be a stampede."

I laughed with her. "No, probably not. That was a little anti climatic."

Another giggle from her as she walked behind the counter, taking her position at the register. "Was it like this at your other bakery?"

I shook my head. "Not really, but I was opening in a larger city on a busy street. There had been a lot of buzz before we opened. The first few days we were slammed and then things tapered off. Fortunately, after a month or so, business picked back up and steadily increased. It took people a while for word to travel. So many cafes and other stores had been in that same space, no one took us seriously at first."

"Tara is going to do great. She seemed pretty excited to take over full-time," she said, referring to my manager for the bakery I'd left behind when I moved.

"Yeah, she'll be fabulous. She's been my assistant for over two years. She's more than ready to run the whole show. I couldn't close it. That store was my baby. I nurtured it for so long, I couldn't let it go."

Daphne flashed a grin. "Now, you're officially a chain!"

I laughed. "I don't know if two bakeries make a chain, but you're a part of that chain as well if they do."

"Divine Desserts will soon be in every city!" Daphne teased.

"Yeah, let's not get ahead of ourselves," I warned.

We both stood behind the counter, waiting for our first customer. I knew the risks of opening a business in a small town, but Daphne was confident we could do it. It wouldn't be a booming business, but I was certain we could make it profitable. I was actually looking forward to the slower pace a small town bakery would offer. I was completely at peace with working eight-hour days instead of twelve or more.

When the first customer walked through the door, we both froze. "Hi," I finally greeted the elderly man who was scrutinizing the cookies in the case.

"Can I offer you a sample?" Daphne volunteered.

The man studied the assortment of cookies and finally settled on a baker's dozen of chocolate chip cookies. Daphne rang him up while I restocked.

"That was kind of intense," I whispered to Daphne once the man was gone. "He didn't look happy, like we forced him to come in and buy cookies."

"That's just Grumpy Gus. Don't you remember him?" she asked.

My eyes widened, "He's still alive?"

That made her giggle. "Yes, he's still alive. He's the town grump and clearly not ready to give up his role anytime soon."

I nodded in understanding. Gus had been old when I was little. That made him close to a relic now. It had been so long since I'd seen him, I hadn't recognized him.

The little bells above the door jingled again. We looked up to see my mother coming through the door. She glanced around the empty bakery before her gaze made its way to us, tension lining her features.

"Slow start?"

"It'll pick up. We've only been open five minutes, after all. People may not even realize we're here yet," I explained, hoping to calm my own nerves as well as Daphne's.

"Well, it's good no one's here. I need to talk to you. Both of you," she said, flicking her eyes between us.

"What's up?" I asked, assuming it was something to do with the coven.

"There's been a theft," she announced.

Daphne and I looked at each other and then back at my mother. "A theft?"

She nodded her head, looked back at the door and then leaned over the counter. "At the museum."

"Lemon Bliss has a museum?" I asked in bewilderment.

My mother rolled her eyes. "Oh good grief, Violet! Do you remember anything from growing up here?"

I looked to Daphne for help. "You know, the old museum. It's really an old house. There isn't too much in there, just stuff that showcases the history of Lemon Bliss," she explained.

"Oh," I said. With her prompt, I recalled visiting the place when we had been in grade school. It was small and only open a day or two a week. It wasn't exactly a main tourist attraction.

"What was stolen?" Daphne asked.

My mother ran one of her hands over her black hair, her bracelets clinking as she smoothed back the stray strands that had fallen loose from the knot atop her head.

"Several items, but two are of serious concern for us. There will be a coven meeting tomorrow night to discuss the issue," she said in a low voice.

"Mom, there's no one here," I reminded her.

"I know that," she shot back, her irritation evident.

Daphne reached out and squeezed my mother's hand. "We'll be there. I'm sure it will be fine. There's nothing to worry about."

"If only that were true," she muttered as she stepped back from the counter.

"Do you want a doughnut or a muffin?" I asked, hoping to nudge her mind off of her worries. I never quite knew how seriously to take my mother. She tended toward dramatic. Only occasionally were her theatric reactions justified.

"No thank you. I need to talk to Lila. I'll see you girls tomorrow, and good luck with your grand opening. I'll be sure to pass along the word that you're open and ready for business," she said, waving as she walked out. The sound of charm bracelets jingling followed her out the door.

"That was weird," Daphne said, once the door fell closed behind my mother. "Virginia is not one to get worked up about anything."

I shrugged a shoulder. "She's still on edge about the death of that supernatural investigator in the factory. She's been waiting for the other shoe to drop for months. I keep telling her we're fine and there's nothing to worry about, but she is convinced she senses something coming."

"Well, I think your mom might be someone I would trust in that department," Daphne said, her brow furrowing. "I just hope it isn't another murder."

We were interrupted when another customer came through the door, followed by a steady stream of people for the next couple of hours. The sales depleted many of the cookies and muffins, which meant it was time to start baking. I loved baking and was more than happy to leave the front of the bakery to Daphne while I put on my apron and got to work.

"Hey," she popped her head in the kitchen a while later.

"Hi. How's it going out there?"

She shook her head. "Ever get what you asked for and then regret it?"

I chuckled as I carefully filled muffin cups with batter. "Yep. Pretty busy out there?"

"We're almost completely wiped out of cookies. I just sold our last blueberry muffin as well."

I nodded and pointed to a cooling rack filled with blueberry muffins. "Those are ready to go. There are peanut butter cookies in the oven, and I'll get started on chocolate chip as soon as I get these in the oven," I replied, entirely in my element.

Daphne nodded and carried the muffins out to the front. I could hear the bells jingle and knew another customer was coming in. That was definitely a good sign.

I spent the next several hours baking muffins and cookies, and fielding questions about the specialty cakes we were offering. Daphne managed to secure several orders, mostly for birthdays, and one anniversary cake. I could feel the strain of the day's business getting to me and couldn't wait to get home and put up my feet.

"Can I kiss the cook?" a deep voice cut through my thoughts just as I was slicing through a piecrust.

I smiled and turned to face Gabriel Trahan. "There you are."

"I stopped by earlier, but poor Daphne looked like she was overwhelmed. I figured I'd come back when things had slowed down," he said, leaning in and giving me a quick kiss.

"It's been busy."

"Here, I thought you could use this," he said, handing me a cup of coffee from Crooked Coffee, my favorite local coffee shop in Lemon Bliss.

"Thank you. Daphne is still planning on moving forward with her coffee shop plan," I laughed. "She may change her mind after today."

"She looks like she might be getting tired. Are you guys going to hire any help?"

"That's the plan, but we wanted to see what we needed. This first month, it will just be the two of us. My mom and her friends have offered to help if we need it. Considering how busy we are on a Tuesday, I think we may need them for this Saturday," I said, sliding a tray of cookies into the oven.

"I'm here for you as well. I may not be as pretty as the ladies, but I can sell a doughnut or two," he said with that familiar grin that never failed to send a curl of warmth through me.

"We might take you up on that, which means you might live to regret it," I countered with a wink.

He chuckled. "I'll let you get back to work. I just wanted to stop by and tell you good luck, but I don't think you need it. I'll call you tonight and you can fill me in on the rest of the day," he said, giving me another quick kiss before slipping out the back door.

I sipped my coffee, savoring the rich flavor and the kick of caffeine. I could've used a second wind, and this might do the trick. I still had tons of baking to prep for tomorrow. We were definitely going to need to hire an assistant. I could keep up for now, but I certainly didn't want to work at this pace forever.

"I'm so tired. I'm going straight home, crawling into a hot bubble bath and drinking a glass of wine," Daphne said as she came through the kitchen door.

"Are we closed?" I asked in surprise.

She nodded. "It's four. We're officially done for the day."

"Oh, now it's time to clean up," I said with a wink.

"Oh no, you're kidding right?"

I shook my head. "We can't leave it looking like this. It won't take long. You take care of the front, and I'll finish up back here."

She was mumbling as she headed out. "Who thought this was a good idea?"

"You did!" I shouted.

Despite the physical exhaustion, I was charged with

energy. The day had been hectic, but I thrived on the adrenaline rush. I knew it wouldn't always be like this. I wanted to cherish the moment, even if I was so tired I could barely stand.

I'd reluctantly returned to Lemon Bliss, Louisiana for what I thought would be a temporary visit several months ago. In short order, I'd learned I was a witch descended from generations of witches, gotten caught up in the investigation of a suspicious murder at the defunct lemon tea factory I'd inherited from my grandmother, and reconnected with a few old friends. I'd come back to my hometown with no intention of staying, only to discover I didn't want to leave.

Hey, I had witchy things to learn. Plus, my old bestie, Daphne, persuaded me that Lemon Bliss was in need of a bakery and we were the ones to make it happen. It was a win for our 'official' opening day to be a success.

I took one last look around the kitchen and declared it was clean and ready to go tomorrow morning. I was going to come in early and get a head start on the baking.

"Ready?" I asked Daphne who was stocking napkins at the counter.

"Yes! Let's get out of here."

We walked out together, locked up and went our separate ways. We were both too tired for chitchat. As I walked to my car, I thought about my mother's visit and how upset she had been. I hoped it wasn't anything serious. I didn't have the time to worry about another threat to the witches in Lemon Bliss.

AVAILABLE NOW!

A Spell To Tell

IF YOU'D LIKE updates when I have new releases and other news, sign up for my newsletter: https://lucymayauthor.com/subscribe

# MY BOOKS

Thank you for reading Witch You Wouldn't Believe! I
hope you enjoyed the magic. If so, here are a few ways to
help other readers find my books.

1) Write a review!
2) Sign up for my newsletter, so you can receive
information on new releases:
https://lucymayauthor.com/subscribe
3) Like my Facebook page at
https://www.facebook.com/lucymayauthor/

\* \* \*

**Lemon Tea Cozy Mysteries**
Witch You Wouldn't Believe
A Spell to Tell
Witch is When it Gets Crazy

**Wicked Good Mystery Series**

Destiny's A Witch - coming August 2018
Hex Me Not - coming October 2018
Spells & Silver Bells - coming December 2018

# ACKNOWLEDGMENTS

So many thanks to give. I'll start with you first - if you're reading this, I hope you enjoyed the story. Thank you! Readers mean the world to me, so thanks for taking a chance.

This book would not have been written without the support of my husband who conveniently believes in magic and wholeheartedly supports me writing whatever stories I want to whip up. Without some of my amazing author friends, I might not have had the courage to spread my wings. Many thanks to Cosmic Letterz for making fun magic with this cover.

Last, but certainly not least, my dogs who spoil me with wags and kisses every day.

xoxo

Lucy May

# ABOUT THE AUTHOR

Lucy May loves coffee, dogs, cooking, and writing. She's a misplaced Southerner living in Maine. She's grown to love four seasons, but she still pines for sleepy southern summers. She likes to think she might've been a witch in another life and still believes in magic. She wiles away her time spinning snarky, witchy & sexy paranormal stories.

**f**

Made in the USA
Columbia, SC
05 July 2020